ESTHOPIA SAGAS
INVASION OF THE ORTAKS

BOOK 6 VIKINGS

SVEINN BENÓNÝSSON

COPYRIGHT

To all of you who love fiction, adventure, and fantasy!

CONTENTS

Esthopia

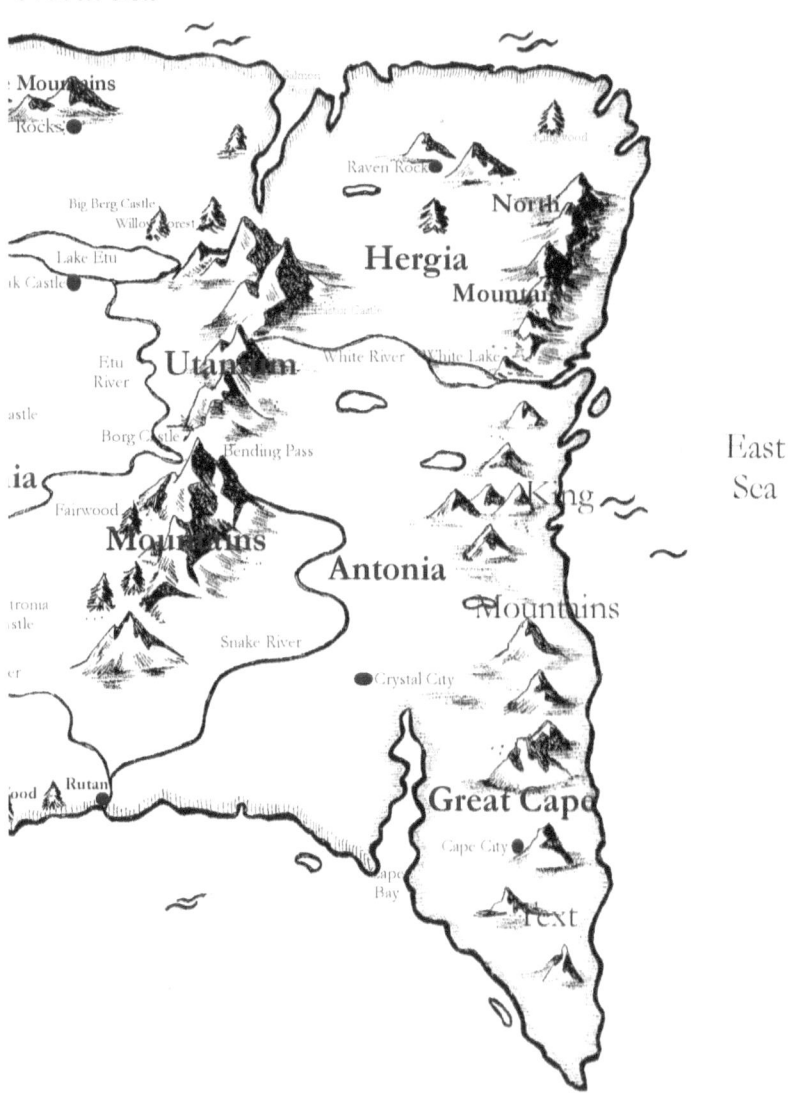

PROLOGUE

*I*t's been two hundred fifty years since the events that are presented here in this writing took place. I have spent most of my life gathering data, which I have applied. In many cases, the recorded data has been lost. In those cases, I have had to rely on stories, which have been passed down orally man-to-man, from father to son. I believe that they are somewhat reliable sources. I have travelled widely in search of this data, ranging from Little Creek in Serpenia to Kingwood in Hergia, and from Crystal City in Antonia to the Hunting Valleys in Northern Esthopia. Although a long time has passed, the stories live within the people.

FROM ENIKTRONIA CASTLE.
    Lord Edward.

1 THREE MESSENGERS

*T*he brown and golden autumn leaves rained down as she rode the paths leading through the woodland in the highlands east of Little Creek.

Victoria wanted to see for herself what her men had reported they found a few days earlier.

Accompanied by seventy well-trained soldiers, she had travelled from Little Creek to investigate. They had been on their journey for two days now, and were heading toward a remote valley that very few, other than the local hunters and her scouts, knew of.

After several hours, she rode up on a hill overlooking the valley, and what she saw was terrifying. The whole valley had obviously been a campsite. There were huts and campfires strewn across the valley.

Tents and small shelters had been erected by the hundreds. Lying on the ground between each of them, or nailed on the walls and doors of the huts, were corpses in large numbers.

She had known what to expect, since her scouts had found this on their expeditions and informed her, but the sight was overwhelming in person.

The terrible smell of rotting corpses filled her nostrils, and she had to struggle not to gag. Some of the huts and the tents had been burned, but most were still standing, fully displaying their ghoulish additions.

She rode down into the campsite, bracing herself for what she was about to experience, but there was no preparing for what she saw.

The bodies were not just of men. There were women and children amongst them, and in some cases, very young children.

Why? What could those children, so very young, have possibly done to deserve this? The complete lack of mercy infuriated her. She became more and more angry as she rode through the campsite. Unfortunately, wolves and other scavengers had started feeding on some of the corpses, desecrating them further, but they fled as soon as they saw the humans approaching.

She stopped her horse at the end of the valley and turned to her men.

"We must burn these corpses, and bury their ashes," she commanded firmly, but her voice revealed how upset she was.

Her men did as instructed, and for the rest of that day, they carried out the unpleasant task of gathering the corpses. By evening, they had made five piles, after which they set them all on fire. They had counted three hundred people who had been killed and left to rot in that campsite.

The next morning they dug a big grave and buried the ashes of those who had died there.

They stood there for a moment in silence, in honour of the people who had lost their lives. Victoria had a hard time holding back the tears she felt burning her eyes, but she managed to keep herself in check, determined to show the leadership that was expected of her. As she stood there, watching the flames die down, she turned her words to one of her scouts.

"Anton, I need you to go to Erinstein Castle for me, and give Governor Jeff a report of what has happened here. Tell him that I will be expecting him in Little Creek for a meeting. Be clear that he should make haste; we need to address this before it spins out of our control." She cleared her throat, her emotion getting the better of her after seeing the children's corpses.

Her scouts had informed her that the people had fled the Ortaks, but unlike those who marched to Goat Valley, they had been followers of one of the outlaws, who had been seeking support to reign in these territories. The outlaw had promised them that he would fight the Ortaks.

Then the campsite was raided by a nobleman, Lord Ferdinand, and his men. She had no idea why or what he had in mind when he had carried out the attack, but her scouts had followed him and his men to his castle two days south from this valley.

Maybe this was his answer to the outlaws who had been raiding his lands. Whatever his reasons, he needed to explain himself. This was not within the law of Serpenia.

Ever since the king and the prince died at the battle of Broad Valley, there had been growing numbers of raids on villages and farms. On top of that, Crown City was far away, and the law enforcement stationed in that city could not do much to protect the lands all the way here in the north.

On top of that, Victoria had been busy building the royal fleet, so her hands were tied. Even with the two hundred men she had to enforce law, it just was not enough. Too many noblemen did not recognise her authority, or the queen.

The north was a vast and hard land. But it was also a fragile land, and had been a great provider for the royal army. It had many small castles and lords, some of whom had followed the king in his warfare and died beside him in the battle. Since the royal family had been killed, there was no one except Queen Egny to take over the throne, and she was now far away in Otanga.

Some of the noblemen, who were able to flee from the battle in Broad Valley, were raising an army in their own favour here in the north. There were many supporting them in their talk of taking over the throne; some of them were growing in strength. They wanted the northern parts of Serpenia to be theirs.

Victoria knew that they were looked at as outlaws and rebels now, but some of them had increased in numbers. With the newfound confidence their supporters provided, they were taking what they called taxes, needed to feed their troops, but that were used to create wealth for themselves.

One of those noblemen was Lord Grimstein, whom her brother had defeated in the early spring, but there were others like him. Rumours of an uprising was reported by her scouts. If the queen did not return soon, a civil war between the noblemen was almost a given, and a new monarch could rise from that.

Victoria knew if something was not done soon to prevent this, it could end badly. So it was important that action be taken to prevent such, if it wasn't too late already.

On top of that, outlaws sought shelter within these lands. Here, they could easily hide in the remote valleys, empty castles, and woodlands.

She stood there, silently thinking, as she watched her scout mounting his horse.

"Anton," she called out, and he approached his captain.

"Take two men with you, and try not to get into any trouble on your way. It is vital that the governor hears what has happened here."

"Yes, Captain," he replied, then he turned his horse and called on two men he knew well.

Victoria watched them leave, winding their way down the valley before they disappeared into the woods. There was nothing more to be done here, so she mounted her horse, and with the rest of her men, she headed for home.

ANTON HAD PICKED the two men he trusted the most to travel with him to Erinstein Castle. Ragnar and his cousin Baldwin were his childhood friends. The three of them were well-trained soldiers, and they knew each other well. All were excellent swordsmen and fine marksmen with their bows.

They were all the same age, in their early thirties, and all wore the same sort of clothing. Brown, studded gambeson, green woollen trousers, and brown leather boots. They were each girded with a sword, a knife had been thrust into each of their black leather belts, and they all had a bow and quiver.

Anton was a bit taller than the other two, but they were all strong and well-built. Spending ample time in the woods since early childhood had made them well aware of any sound or smell in the woodlands.

They had all been raised in a small village close to Little Creek, and most of their childhood was spent hunting all kinds of animals. They had learned early how to sneak up on their prey, and live off the land. They were now in their old hunting grounds; they knew these woods like the backs of their hands.

Like Lord Axel, they had all joined the army and their king to face the Ortaks at Broad Valley, and like Axel, they barely managed to escape death on their flight from the battlefield. They had stuck together, while finding their way back to their homeland, and they had been some of the first to join Axel and Jeff by the cabin in Green Woods. Their families had marched with them to Goat Valley, where they could be safe from the Ortaks and the war.

With their background and upbringing, they were all ideal scouts. They had joined Axel and his rebellion army, when he headed out from Goat Valley to fight the Ortaks last winter.

Now they made their way toward Erinstein Castle, bringing the news from their captain, Victoria.

They tried to stay out of people's way by keeping themselves on less-travelled paths. This would take them a bit longer, but they would be in great danger if spotted by Lord Ferdinand's men, so the extra time was more than worth it.

They estimated that it would take them at least four days to reach their destination. Taking the high lands across the wilderness, it felt colder, as autumn had arrived, chasing away the warmth of the summer.

They saw no one on their first day, and at nightfall, they camped in an area where they had done so many times before. They did not speak a word, but listened and looked around quietly, knowing that there might be scouts in the area.

They rested well that night, but it was cold, as the first snow of winter blanketed the high land. They managed to light a small fire to warm themselves, before heading off again.

By midday, the autumn sun had melted most of the snow, and as the path took them down from the high land again, the sun warmed them up. They stopped in a clearing overlooking the terrain ahead to rest the horses, then they continued their journey.

They managed to hunt a deer later that day, and the fresh meat, lightened their mood by the campfire that evening. The next morning they were on their way by daybreak.

After three hours of riding through the woodland that day, they stopped by a river crossing. They dismounted, so the horses could drink.

The weather was getting colder again, and as they stood on the riverbank, Anton took a deep breath and looked up into the sky.

"I think it's going to rain soon," he said. The others nodded their agreement.

"We are being followed," said Ragnar, keeping his voice down.

"They have been on our heels for an hour," said Baldwin as he picked up his horse's reins, which had dropped while the horse drank.

Anton nodded. "At least four of them, possibly five."

"I counted five, about twenty minutes behind us," said Ragnar.

"I counted five too, so . . . what do we do?" Baldwin looked at Anton.

"We should head down the river, to the village," he replied, as he mounted his horse. They headed off again, but this time, they travelled at a faster pace. They rode through the woodland, crossing small streams and rough terrain, as they tried to get a bigger gap between them and their followers. By midday they approached an area they knew well. Here, the river snaked between high, rocky hills, where it eventually emerged into a grassy flatland near Sunny Pastures.

They rode into the river and kept heading downstream. They knew that they had put a good distance between themselves and their followers, and were hoping to lose them completely by disguising their tracks in the water.

They rode down the river as fast as they could, and when they reached the place where the hills ended and the flatland lay ahead, they took a turn to the right. Once they emerged from the river, they stopped by a group of bushes, where they dismounted and tied their horses. With their horses secured, they ran up the hilltop, where they had a good view of the river.

They placed themselves a few metres apart and hid behind a big tree that had fallen at the edge of the cliff. Anton took his place in the middle, with Ragnar at his right, and Baldwin to his left. Then they waited.

It was about twenty minutes later that Ragnar noticed a movement on the other bank of the river. They raised their heads, and sat there perfectly still, watching the other side, when a herd of reindeer approached. Carefully, they raised themselves up high enough to have a good view. Then, suddenly, a big stag walked out from the woodland and stopped at the edge of the opposite bank of the river.

That beautiful animal just stood there looking straight at them with no sign of fear, as if it knew that they could not hunt it at this time. Then, after a while, he turned and gracefully led his herd down the slope, and they watched how they ran carelessly into the pastures.

The three men looked at each other. This was an unusual experience for them, having such game within their reach, without being able to shoot it.

They hid themselves again, and waited for those who followed. About half an hour later, the first rider emerged from behind the bend, and another one beside him.

They had their bows in their hands, with arrows already in place in them, ready to shoot in case of an ambush. They were very careful as they rode slowly down the stream, looking on both sides.

Anton gave the others a signal to let them pass. He knew there were more of them who had not yet shown themselves, and he wanted them all in the open before making his move.

Shortly afterwards, the last three came around the bend, one by one in a row, and like the first two, they were prepared for an ambush, holding their bows at the ready, and looking around as they rode downstream.

When they were straight down from Anton, he gave the order by nodding his head, then, in one swift move, he raised himself and his bow, and shot the man in the middle straight in the heart.

Baldwin shot his arrow at the man riding first, hitting him in the shoulder, but the man was faster, and quickly shot a return arrow. The arrow landed in Baldwin's left thigh. As he released his arrow, the man fell off his horse and into the water.Ragnar shot him when he stood up. The arrow hit him in his right shoulder, and he fell backward onto the ground.

By that time, Anton had another arrow in his bow, but the man he was aiming at had jumped off his horse, keeping himself hidden behind it. A few seconds later, he lifted his bow to shoot, but Anton had been waiting for him to make a move, and as soon as he raised his head from behind the horse, Anton shot him straight in the forehead.

He then swiftly moved behind a tree, as an arrow coming from the other direction slammed into the bark in the exact spot where he had been standing. The other two who had been riding up front had returned.

Baldwin, despite the arrow in his thigh, returned the shot with one of his own, but his arrow missed, passing by one of the men, barely avoiding hitting him in the face.

The two were still on horseback, and now turned away from the ambush. They rode as fast as they could, heading downstream. Anton raised his bow again and took good aim. His arrow hit the man on the right side straight in the back, but somehow, the man managed to stay on his horse and keep on riding.

They watched them as they rode down the river at a great speed for a while, before turning left, urging their mounts out of the river, then eventually disappearing behind the bushes.

Anton placed another arrow in his bow, looking down into the river at the man who had shot Baldwin, but the man now floated with his face down in the water. He was obviously dead, so he lowered the bow and placed the arrow back in his quiver.

He saw that Baldwin was leaning against a tree, holding his hand above the arrow that jutted from his thigh. He turned to see Ragnar still on the ground, moaning. He looked seriously wounded, with the arrow through his shoulder.

He bent down to have a better look, and saw that the arrow was quite low, but not all the way through. *Too close to the heart,* he thought.

He raised himself up again and turned to Baldwin.

"We need to remove those arrows, and seal your wounds before you get an infection," he told him. Then he stood there for a moment, thinking. "Can you manage to get down to the horses, if I help Ragnar down the slope?" Baldwin nodded and started limping down the slope.

Anton bent down close to his friends. He took his knife from its sheath and cut out a big piece of Ragnar's shirt, then he dragged the arrow from his shoulder, and quickly tied the piece of shirt tightly around his shoulder, to stop the bleeding. He took his belt to bind the wound, tightening it as far as possible. Ragnar fainted. He picked his friend up and carried him down the slope.

Baldwin was already there, lying on the ground by the horses. Anton lay Ragnar down, then he gathered some firewood and lit a campfire, placing his knife on the flames.

He turned to Baldwin, and with a firm and steady hand, he swiftly removed the arrow from his thigh.

After sealing and binding both wounds, he stood there looking at them as they lay with their heads up against a tree.

"It's not too late. There is still time remaining of the day, enough for me to reach the village and get some help before dark." He looked around. Ragnar had lost consciousness again. Baldwin was in great pain but nodded. "I will be back with men to help and two stretchers to take you to the village," he said as he mounted his horse.

There was no sign of the two men who had fled the ambush. He figured that the one he shot was either dead, or severely wounded.

Whichever it was, he had no time to think of that now. He had to get to the village as soon as possible. He rode as fast as he could across the pastures, and over to the hilly woodland on the other side. It was the shortest way to the village, which was down by a small, peaceful lake on the other side of the woods.

He knew it would only take him an hour and a half to ride through the woods, if he stayed on the path.

Worried more about his friends than being cautious, he was too careless. He rushed in great speed through the woodland, staying strictly on the leaf-covered path that after-noon. He was in deep thought, worrying about his friends as they lay wounded in the bushes, so he didn't see the arrow until it was too late.

For one split second, he saw the archer standing in front of him on the path, holding the bow in his hand, as the arrow penetrated his heart. Then he rolled backward out of the saddle, landing on his back. He felt no pain, but saw the trees and the branches reaching out to the sky, before all went black.

BALDWIN WATCHED his friend hurry off, having no choice but to leave them lying helpless on the ground.

Ragnar was still unconscious, and he had not seen his friend's chest move for a while, so he inched himself closer to him, despite the pain in his thigh, which was getting worse.

He put his hand on Ragnar's chest, hoping to feel his

heartbeat, but there was none. Then he pressed his fingers on his neck to see if he could find a pulse, but he found none. Ragnar was cold, pale, and his lips were blue, and turning white.

He had to face the fact that his friend was dead. His kin, a close friend since early childhood, was dead. His tears started to fall, and he had no control of his grief. He just sat there almost paralysed, looking at the body with his empty eyes.

Then he managed to pull himself together, and looking around, he realised it would be dark soon, and there was no sign of Anton yet.

Maybe too soon to be expecting that, he thought as he wiped the tears from his cheeks and cleared his throat, but he had a strange feeling that something was wrong.

He thought for a moment, reviewing his situation, and he realised that he was an easy target here. If their enemies returned, they would see him with ease.

Hence he covered more of Ragnar's body with his blanket, then he raised himself up, gritting his teeth against the terrible pain in his thigh.

He placed some pieces of wood on the ground where he had been resting since Anton left, and then he covered it with his own blanket, making it look like someone was sleeping there. Then he placed more wood on the fire, and he limped behind the tree, hiding himself in the bushes.

He had only been there for half an hour before the sun began to set, and within moments, he saw a man approaching through the pastures on horseback.

He recognised the man as the one who had been riding in the front at the ambush. He was obviously coming to finish them off.

He briefly wondered what had happened to Anton, but then started worrying about himself as he saw the man dismount his horse, about fifty metres away.

It was getting darker by the minute, but he was able to see the man sneaking slowly forward with his bow in his hand, coming closer and closer to the campsite.

The man stopped for a while, to listen and watch what he thought to be the two men sleeping, then he came closer. Baldwin drew his sword slowly, and without making any sound, continued watching the man the whole time.

Suddenly, the attacker shot his arrow into Ragnar's body, then he drew another arrow and shot the pile of firewood that he thought to be Baldwin.

As soon as he shot the second arrow, and in spite of the pain, Baldwin jumped from the bushes with his sword in his hand.

The attacker swiftly moved away from the blow and let go of his bow, then drew his own sword. By that time, Baldwin had thrust his sword out again, hitting the man in his left hand, pleased when he screamed out.

The attacker answered with a blow of his own that Baldwin managed to block, immediately lashing out at the man, landing a good blow in the face with his left hand. He finished the fight by stabbing the man swiftly in the heart. The man looked surprised, then he fell facedown.

Baldwin stood there for a moment, realising that he had forgotten his pain in all the excitement of the fight. He made up his mind, and walked to his horse. After a few minutes he had saddled the horse and managed to mount. He was going to the village to have someone fetch the bodies, and then he would keep on his journey to Erinstein Castle and deliver the message from his captain to his governor, as directed.

It had been a long summer at Storm Castle in Eniktronia, as Lord Gesner grieved his sons. His grief was reflected in his work as governor for the region.

That summer he received a letter from the queen, where she expressed her deepest condolences and hoped for his loyalty. It was some consolation, and it gave him some strength in his sorrow. Then, before the autumn set in, the news of Big John's death arrived with a messenger from Lord Klaus at Borg Castle. His lordship was furious at the news.

Not only had he known the man, as Big John had spent the last winter at his castle, but he had also helped his life-long friend when he had almost been eaten by a savage beast. He was also angry at himself, for not having Crown Castle rebuilt and garrisoned, to keep law and order on the Heath.

The news came as a shock to Sir William.

"Big John was a noble man, and a true friend," he said to His Lordship.

"We will honour that man, and those still living—Crown Castle must be rebuilt," said His Lordship in a deep voice, almost as if talking to himself. "How is your leg, my friend? Do you think you can ride a horse?" he asked Sir William.

"Much better after I started walking and moving about," he replied as he slapped his hand on the wounded thigh. "What does His Lordship have in mind? I'm not sure about the horse riding, though, as I haven't tried that yet. Still using a stick—well, a spear, to be precise. Other than that, I am at Your Lordship's service." He bowed a little.

His Lordship smiled.

"I am glad you're recovering, my friend. I have a task for

you." His Lordship stood up from his chair and walked to the window overlooking the bailey. His men were practicing their skills, and there was a change of shifts at the castle guard.

"It would do you some good to return to Crown Castle and take charge in rebuilding it," he said, and turned his head toward his friend. "I will send Sir Alfred of Ternesholt with you. He will be in charge of the military and law enforcement on the Heath."

"Yes, Your Lordship, it will do me good to get back and start rebuilding." Sir William cast his eyes on the castle floor.

Although he was glad to be of service, he was also worried. The memory of those beasts had haunted him, both in his dreams and while awake.

But he was a knight and a soldier. He had seen many things he did not want to see, and he just had to brush this off the same as he had the rest. That is what knights do, as he had learned while still a young man.

His Lordship turned from the window.

"You should start preparing for your trip. I will provide you with workers, so you can get the job done, and Sir Alfred will escort you with his men," ordered His Lordship, then he walked out of the hall and returned to his chambers.

Three days later, His Lordship watched from the wall of his castle as Sir William and Sir Ternesholt headed off from Storm Castle with fifty workers and one hundred soldiers, toward Crown Castle.

2 VIKINGS LANDING

*K*ing Haldor The White, as he was called, stood in the prow of his longship at daybreak. He had made a bold decision.

To leave his homeland and sail south to the lands of plenty, as his people had called those lands since his early childhood, was not an easy choice to make. Accompanying him as a co-leader on this voyage was his right hand and half brother, Oskar The Black.

King Haldor The White was known for his wisdom and courage. He was medium in height, bald-headed, with a long brown beard. He was in his early thirties. The bow was his weapon of choice, but he also had a short sword and a big hunting knife girded in the belt around his waist. All were weapons that he was quite skilled to use. His wife, Ragna, was a proud woman, and they had two sons, Gudvar, who was ten years old, and Sigmund, who was eight.

His half brother was a big, strong man. A bit younger than the king, his black hair lay down his back, and his beard flowed down to his broad chest. The big two-bladed battle-axe was his preferred weapon. His wife was Brynja, and they had three daughters between the ages of nine and three.

The two men had been inseparable since early childhood. No one who had fought against the two of them had lived.

Rumours and stories were of lands within ten days' sailing to the South. Those were said to be vast lands and fertile. There, they could create a new home for themselves and their people, who were growing in numbers.

Stories had been told of this land over the campfires in the wintertime for many years.

The king and most others had always thought of it as tales for fun, just to pass the time during long, dark winter evenings by the fire.

Then, one day, early autumn, a ship arrived at their shore. It had been carried north by strong winds, with a broken wheel leaving them unable to steer.

The crew on this ship were not of his kingdom, but were merchants from the lands in the south. Their captain's name was Richard. He was a thin, tall man, with a strange gaze in his eyes, like he was hiding something. He was always on the alert, from someone or something.

The king had a hard time trusting him, but after long conversations with him and his crew over the course of that winter, the king was finally convinced that there were such lands as he had always heard of.

He had learned from these men that the lands were called Esthopia. His men searched their ship, and found a map, which showed six kingdoms, and according to the captain, there were five of them in peace and bound by family ties.

But one of them had no such ties, and that kingdom was in the most north-eastern part of the lands.

It was called Hergia. That was where he was now headed.

For some years, a king from the northern fjords and valleys had grown in strength, and he had gained more and more and more lands.

That king was King Kostmund. His expansion was beginning to be a threat for King Haldor and his people. This could easily end in battle, and there would be a great loss of men on both sides.

That gave him a reason to leave and head south. His curiosity and thirst for new adventures overtook him, when he heard the stories that the crew of this lost ship told him. He saw an opportunity to raise sails, and look for new lands. There was no downside, or so he told himself.

So the following spring, he rode off, along with his closest allies, to a meeting with King Kostmund. That meeting led to a peace treaty, granting him six months to prepare for his voyage.

News of the king leaving travelled fast in the fjords and valleys, and as time went by that summer, more and more noblemen and common farmers, who had followed him in his battles, announced their loyalty to him, and were willing to leave with their own families and sail with him on his journey across the sea.

And at the end of that summer, when his treaty had expired, they had all set their livestock and their families on board their longships.

So one autumn morning, four hundred ships left the coast and headed out to the open sea. They steamed south to the promised lands, bringing the merchants with him on his ship, to help guide them on their way. King Harold was convinced he would get to Esthopia, and Richard would lead them to good lands for him and his people.

But he was also beginning to worry. He had seen how the autumn leaves were piling up on the houses, and the snow in the mountains was telling him that the winter was coming, and there was no time to waste.

The autumn storms could come at any moment now. That could have a devastating effect on the fleet, if it hit them while they were still at sea.

But strong northern winds carried them safely south across the waters. For five days, there was only the endless ocean to be seen, and their longships sailed the waters, heading farther and farther away from their homelands.

Fear was beginning to set in, as the wind filled their sails, carrying them across the waves.

Then, early in the morning on the sixth day, they finally saw land ahead, and as the lands of Esthopia drew nearer, his heart beat faster.

It was not until evening that day, that the fleet reached the shores of Hergia. They landed three days' ride east of Salmon Fjord.

The king stepped ashore onto the beach, his heart pounding with excitement. In front of him was a green, grassy valley, surrounded by high green hills and pastures.

Few trees dotted the hillsides, but farther in the south, he saw woodland, and above that, mountaintops. The merchants told him that on the other side of those mountains lay the royal city, Raven Rock.

The day was almost at its end, so he and his crew made camp, waiting for the other ships as they approached the shores.

He had his men raising him a tent in the valley, and a fence around the campsite, then his men dug a ditch for defence.

The king walked up the hillside to take a better look at the lands, and he smiled. He could see the mountains in the south turning red in the twilight, and as the darkness settled over the land, he saw villages that were by the seaside and up in the valleys. They lit up as the night cast its shadow over these peaceful lands, and the campfires where his men had camped for the night.

This is home, he thought, as he walked back down the hillside and made his way into his tent.

Early the next morning the king stepped out from his tent, and took a deep breath as he inhaled the air coming from the mountains in the south. Oskar The Black had landed in the next valley to the west.

The longships were now being unloaded onto the beaches, and it took their men two days to unload the whole fleet. Soon, though, all four hundred longships were cared for, with the people and livestock up on land.

The king sent three ships to explore the coast, and the lands in the east. They were to go as far as White River. And another three ships were sent to the west, to explore the lands in Hergia, and into Salmon Fjord. Then he sent scouts in all directions to give him reports on whether there was any threat of war with King Oswald.

In the afternoon, the king went for a walk with his closest followers, as well as Richard the merchant. He wanted to get a better look of the area in the daylight. He came upon the bank east of the small valley he had landed in. He saw a vast grassy pasture that reached all the way to the woodland in the south, and at least two kilometres to the east. From that high bank, he had a great view to the ocean and the beaches in all directions.

He turned to his men.

"This is where I will have my castle. This is my home now," he said with a smile.

After consulting with his half brother, the king decided to make two strongholds, one for himself, and one for Oskar, where he had landed his ship.

He would stay in one, and Oskar would be in charge of the one in the west valley.

Then their men started to raise their king a stronghold upon the bank. And Oskar's men did the same for him, on a flat pasture in the valley he had landed in. The two strongholds lay a mere half day's ride apart.

They dug moats and raised ramparts in huge circles. There were gates in all the cardinal directions of those ramparts, and drawbridges were laid over the moats by the gates.

Inside each stronghold were twelve longhouses; they were raised by the main streets that lay through them. The streets led from one gate to the other, creating a cross, with a central square in the middle, where they raised the biggest house for their master, the castle.

Smaller houses were soon constructed for workers, and barns for the livestock, along with stables, within the strongholds by the ramparts. From early morning to midnight the king's men worked, eager to complete their new cities.

Three weeks later they had almost met their goal, and they started building a port for their ships, with three piers, for landing and unloading men and merchandise.

King Harold had only been there for ten days, when he was

informed of the Ortaks in Salmon Fjord, a foreign enemy force led by King Armus of Orknia. His scouts had come across them as they investigated the mountains in the west. He had just moved into his newly built longhouse, or castle, in the middle of his stronghold. He looked at Richard with discontent.

"You never mentioned Ortaks. There was no such thing said to my ears," he complained, as he sat down on his throne, which his men had brought with them as they left their homelands. It had been carefully placed inside his new house, on a platform at the very end of the hall.

"No, my lord, I did not think that mattered. Anyway, they had been beaten in Serpenia, about the time we sailed, so I thought they would be gone by now."

The king frowned, and turned his words to his scout.

"How many are they?"

"Hard to tell exactly, but we estimate them to be around four thousand."

"Where exactly are they?"

"They are in a remote valley, six days' walk from here. At this moment, they are finishing raising a stronghold, and are obviously waiting for next spring, or reinforcement, my lord."

"We cannot wait for that, my king." Oskar stepped forward, as he had been listening to the scout's report.

"What do you suggest we do, then?" The king was not happy with this news at all.

"I will take ten thousand men with me, and we will finish them off, now. If we do not, we will be facing two enemies with the coming spring." Oskar looked at the men attending this meeting in the king's longhouse, as if seeking their support.

The king sat there quiet for a while, thinking over what Oskar had suggested.

"All right, then, Oskar. Take your men and march for the Ortaks. I will wait here for news from King Oswald of Hergia. We do not want him to sneak up on us while we deal with the Ortaks," said the king, and waited until Oskar left with his followers, before turning to Richard again, who stood there confused and frightened.

"This you could have told me before I sailed with my people to these lands."

"Yes, Your Lordship, but like—"

"Quiet!" shouted the king.

"You will remain here in my custody, while Oskar and his men deal with the Ortaks, then I will decide what to do with you," said the king as he gave his guards a signal to arrest the merchant.

LEADING an army of one hundred Elves and one hundred Barbarians into the cave of Utanium Mountains in Black Woods, Arthenth and Ylfa were brought into a great hall that seemed to be an armoury and a meeting hall for the Underworld Army. Then they had made their way into Mannheim, the world of men, and then into Alfheim, the world of Elves.

Now, they marched straight ahead, carefully making their way toward a stairway that their scouts had told them about, which lay farther down in the Underworld.

They stopped when they reached the top of the stairway, looking around as if for the last time, trying to convince themselves that they were not going into an ambush, before they headed down the stairs.

The stairway was about five metres wide, and not too steep. At first they were in a tunnel. The walls were moist and slimy, and a strong draft came from down below, telling them that they were about to reach some sort of outside area, where there was wind. They lit an Elven light, so the others were able to see where they were going.

After a while they reached the spot where the staircase opened up, and they stepped onto a landing high on a mountainside. The stairs led to the left, where there was a high straight wall down, and the staircase had been carved out from a mountainside. The straight mountain cliff raised above them as high as they could see.

Looking straight ahead, they saw something that they had a hard time comprehending. Below them was a landscape that lay before their eyes. Dark it was, and as far as they could see, there were mountains, dark rivers, lakes, hills, and cliffs, but the whole landscape was all under a shadow. There was no sunshine, and clouds, dark, some different shades of purple, loomed overhead, while lightning streaked across the sky every now and then.

They stopped for a while, just to gaze over everything they were seeing, watching for movement. But all they saw were big birds of some sort flying over the hills in the far distance.

Arthenth and Ylfa looked at each other carefully, then they turned and continued down the stairs.

The stairs took a turn to the right, as they reached the end of the cliff. Then the stairs became somewhat steeper, and finally ended on the surface that was a part of the landscape.

After walking a while, they saw in the distance, some sort of ruins on a hillside. They decided to walk over, hoping they could use the ruins to hide, and rest for a while. And maybe they would have a good view over the terrain from that hill, to see where they should be heading next.

They walked across a flat surface that ended at a rocky hillside, but a wide, old road took them all the way into the ruins.

The found themselves in huge hallways and amongst pillars that had been used to hold up a roof over all they were looking at, a long, long time ago. While examining the ruins, they realised that it was bigger than they had originally thought.

It was at least five hundred metres wide and one kilometre long. At some point, they realised this must have been a huge palace, but for whom? They could not imagine the beasts they had fought would have any use for what must have been here a long time ago. This was a puzzle.

They split up, and placed guards on every corner of this large ruins, to make sure that no one would be able to sneak up on them, if attacked. But there was no indication of that so far; in fact, there was no one around to be afraid of.

After a while, they lowered their weapons and took a better look around, once they had made sure that they were alone.

In the middle of the ruins was a large, flat surface. *This must have been a garden or a meeting hall of some sort*, thought Ylfa, as she looked around. They gave their men an order to raise a camp there.

"This reminds me of an Elven palace," said Arthenth as he stood there beside her in the middle of the ruins, his hand on his hips, still looking around.

They walked over to what seemed to have been a wall, or what was left of it, to give their men the space they needed to set up camp.

"Exactly what I thought," said Ylfa, as she took some of her food from her bag, and sat down to eat.

"Do you think Elves have raised this and lived here?"

She nodded.

"This has been deserted for a very long time," said Arthenth.

"Well, as you see, the structure of those buildings indicate that Elves built this. And here is the only spot that we have seen where there is something green. Even if it is only moss and grass, it tells me something good has been here," said Ylfa, then she put a piece of dried meat in her mouth.

"You're right. I was wondering about that. I think there is still something good down here. I don't know what it is, but the Demons of the Underworld did not make this, or the greenery." He sat down beside her and began to eat himself, suddenly discovering how hungry he was. Then he took up a piece of paper, and started to write his report to his princess.

He called out to one of his men, and handed him the letter.

"You are to hand this directly to Princess Tania, and no one else."

The messenger bowed a little and headed off toward the stairs. Ylfa raised her hand, and one of the Barbarians took his weapons and went along with the Elven messenger.

"We must not send our men alone. This is a dangerous journey," she said, and picked up her bow. "I will take the first watch myself. We all need to rest for the night, if there is a night and day down here," she said as she headed off to her post as guard.

Arthenth nodded. He gave his men orders to stand watch, and took the first watch himself, but he took another post, separate from Ylfa's. He sensed that she needed to be alone.

He stood there on a big rock that had been a part of a building, or a wall overlooking the wilderness that seemed endless. Dark and mysterious, and ever since he stepped out of the mountain cave, his ears sensed a sound coming from a far distance, a strange sound, like some sort of thunder.

He suddenly turned. He was sure he heard someone, or something, behind him, but there was nothing to be seen.

He stood there listening, but all he heard now was the snoring from the Barbarians as they slept.

He turned again, but slowly, realising there was something amongst them. There was something, or someone, in the ruins that could not be seen.

As Ylfa had expected, there was no night or day. According to the time it had taken them to go through the cave, it should be night now, and he could feel that his body needed rest, but there was this light that seemed as if it would remain indefinitely, as it was late evening. No sunshine, therefore no shadows.

There it was once again. This time it was some five metres to his right, and again, he saw nothing, but he kept his hand on his sword, just in case.

By the end of his watch, he went to his men to lie down. And as he reached them, Ylfa approached him with slow steps, looking all around.

"There is someone among us," she said in a low voice.

He nodded, and they looked at each other. Then, suddenly, for no reason, Ylfa reached out her left hand in a quick move. It even came as a surprise to Arthenth, so quick she was. It seemed she had grabbed something, and she was struggling, but did not let go. She grabbed her knife with her right hand and raised it as if she was going to stab someone, or something.

"Don't stab me!" someone called out, then whatever Ylfa was holding, suddenly appeared before their eyes.

It was a man wearing bright-coloured clothing, and a cape decorated in flowers. The man had fallen to the ground, and his hand was raised above his head, trying to defend himself from the knife Ylfa was yielding.

It was an elderly man, obviously an Elf, but his clothing indicated that he was a sorcerer of some kind, possibly even a necromancer.

"Who are you?" Ylfa was angry.

"I'm Trinserant, and I mean you no harm!" he called out.

"Why do you sneak up on us?" Arthenth asked. He had drawn his sword, when the man had appeared.

"I live here. This is my home, and if you let go of my cape so I can stand up, I will tell you all you want to know," the old man said with a leery look at Ylfa.

"Before she does that . . . " Arthenth gave ten of his men, who had gathered to see what was happening, an order, and they made a tight circle around them. "Just want to be sure you won't be able to disappear and escape from us again," he said as he sheathed his sword. "Now she can let go of your cape, sir."

He stood up slowly and looked intently at them. "You are not from the same tribe. Are you?" he looked at Ylfa for a while with searching eyes. "You must be a Barbarian, are you not? You are certainly not an Elf."

"Before we answer your questions, you will have to

answer ours, old man." Arthenth gazed at him, trying to figure out why he would be here.

"All right, you have the knife on me, so be it, then," said the old man with a little grin.

"Are you alone in these ruins, or do we have to look out for more of your kind in here?" asked Arthenth.

"Well, you can look all you want, but there is only one of me in here, and that is the way it has been for a very long time now," replied the old man, as he sat down on a big rock by his feet. "Excuse me, but my feet are not as they once were," he mumbled.

"Then tell us why you are here." Ylfa was getting impatient.

"Well, it is a long story, but if you insist. I'm an Elf, or I was born as an Elf, to be more exact. I was born with the capability to make myself disappear, and as I grew older, to make others disappear as well. Having such a capability as a young man can be more of a burden than a gift. I became arrogant and distant from others.

"Finally, my family and the few friends I had, had enough of my attitude and abandoned me, or to be more accurate, I abandoned them. That is when I met a necromancer, an elderly man, who took me in and taught me how to use my *gift*, as he called it.

"He took me to the gathering of other necromancers, and I found myself among those who were able to use their capabilities as they chose, and to learn from each other to get stronger and stronger. Ten years later I travelled with a large number of necromancers down to this place. Here, where we all are now." He paused for a moment before he continued with his speech.

"That was a long time ago. We travelled through these

lands amongst the Demons and the beasts, and met many Dark Elves. But when I learned that they had plans of invading and taking over the lands of Elves, I started to question my path.

"A few years later, I decided to make myself disappear for good. I found this place, these ruins, and I have been here ever since. Only a few families of Dark Elves know of me here, and they bring me what I need to get by, but otherwise, I am quite alone." The old man looked up. He had been staring down at the ground the whole time he made his speech.

"What is this place, and why does it remind me of an Elven Palace?" Arthenth looked around once more, as if to make a point.

"Because it *is* an Elven Palace!" Trinserant called out, raising his hands. "This, what you see here, this world, used to be a part of Alfheim!" He lowered his voice. "Before the dark lords overtook these lands, this was a part of Alfheim.

"That was a long, long time ago. Elves used to live here. Then the dark forces rose from the Underworld, and defeated the army of Elves. Ever since that day the dark forces have reigned here." They could hear the sorrow in his voice.

"Do you mean to tell us, this is part of Alfheim, and not the Underworld?" Ylfa looked surprised.

The old man nodded.

They went quiet for a moment, digesting the information they just received. How were they to know that this changed everything?

"Where is the Underworld, then?" Ylfa asked in a low voice, almost afraid to ask.

"The Underworld, as you call it, is a long way from here,

and way down below all this," Trinserant replied. He was beginning to be more relaxed, as he realised that they were not going to kill or harm him.

"Have you seen it?" asked Arthenth.

"No, no one can see the Underworld, no one alive that is, though some say you go there when you're dead. The Underworld is the source and the place of evil!" he replied, his eyes widening past the point one would think they could.

Ylfa and Arthenth looked at each other. This was more information than they had hoped for, and it needed to be delivered to their royalties.

"We will not harm you, old man, but we will have to contain you until you have told us everything. I hope you don't mind that," said Arthenth as he gave two of his men a signal. They bound Trinserant's feet with ropes, so he couldn't run off, then four men took watch over him.

"You will stab him if he makes himself disappear," ordered Arthenth.

He gave Ylfa a signal, and the two of them stepped aside to discuss the matter.

"Do you think he's telling us the truth?" Arthenth looked worried.

"I have no reason to doubt him, and the explanation he gave us, of this being a part of Alfheim, explained a lot," she replied as she looked around the ruins, then she turned questioning eyes back to Arthenth.

"What now?" she asked.

"We question him some more before we send our report," replied Arthenth.

She nodded.

They returned to where they had left Trinserant in the hands of four guards.

"You said you could make others disappear as well." Ylfa sounded sceptical.

But she had hardly said the last word, when the four Elves guarding him vanished into thin air. Ylfa and Arthenth looked at each other. *Show off,* thought Ylfa.

"Bring them back!" Arthenth was not amused by this display, and his men emerged again, looking a bit scared.

"You must have seen the Underworld Army, as they went up the stairs and into the cave, did you not?" Arthenth was still angry at him for making his men disappear.

"Yes, I saw the army as you call it. For weeks, they went by here on the grounds below, and up the stairway into the cave. I have never seen so many of them before. I hid myself away from them, and many times they came up here to search for the one who made this green, but they never found me."

"Did you know they were heading for Alfheim?"

"No, but I guessed it to be." He looked down again. "And since you are here, I presume they did not prevail this time," he added in a low voice. He looked shameful sitting there.

"What more can you tell us of this world? Where do we find the Dark Elves' homes, and where do the Vargs and other creatures keep themselves?"

"About five days from here in this direction"—he pointed straight ahead—"there is a city where most of the Dark Elves keep themselves. It is called Gruntentorg. It is their city, their castle, and their main fortress. Then, there are many other smaller towns and villages, most of them behind those mountains over there, on their left side." He pointed in the direction of the mountains.

"Gruntentorg? Where have I heard that before?" Arthenth was obviously in deep thought.

"You have heard of it in the Elven folk tales, my good man," said Trinserant, smiling. Arthenth nodded; he remembered all the tales told to him as a child.

"We should make our report now and get some rest. We will head out early," said Arthenth as he turned to Ylfa.

"You should not go any farther. There are still strong forces out there, and there are too few of you." The old man looked at them alternately, and they could see that he was scared.

They stood there silent for a while, thinking, then Ylfa turned to Arthenth.

"There seems to be no late or early, but yes, we should make a report. Then we should rest here, and wait for further instructions before continuing. He might be right." For the second time he thought he saw a smile on her face, even though it was brief.

Arthenth nodded. She was right, they should wait for further orders.

Who knows what is out there, he thought and took a look over the landscape once again. As she walked back to the spot where they had stood during their earlier conversation, he followed. They sat down to write out their reports. There was something about this woman that made him feel safe, warm, and content.

When they had finished their reports, they went to the place inside the ruins where their men had camped. The reports were handed over to one Elf and one Barbarian. They watched as they went toward the stairs that led up to the cave in the mountain across the step.

It was time to rest. Arthenth looked around, thinking and trying to visualise the life that had been here within this palace before it was overtaken by evil. Then he lay down to rest.

It will take at least three days before new orders will arrive, and we can use that time to get more information from Trinserant, he thought as he fell asleep.

OSKAR THE BLACK and his men, ten thousand strong, kept themselves close to the beach as they made their way along Salmon Fjord and toward the Ortaks stronghold.

When the beaches were blocked by the high, rocky cliffs reaching into the ocean, they turned to the woodlands and crossed the hills. Taking the longer route, it was not until the sixth day that they reached the valley where the stronghold was.

By that time the Ortaks scouts had informed their commander of the large army of Vikings approaching.

Commander Orthar ordered all his men inside the stronghold.

Those Vikings will not dare to attack our stronghold. We are too many, he thought.

It was early morning when the Vikings approached over the hills and entered the valley from the North. They seemed to be in no hurry.

The first to arrive crossed the pastures and took their stand against the stronghold's main gate, and then, as they grew in numbers, they started to surround the Ortaks stronghold, until it was completely confined by ten thousand men strong.

The Vikings kept themselves out of reach from the Ortaks' arrows. Then they started to prepare for their attack.

Commander Orthar placed himself up on a watchtower overlooking the valley when he heard that the Vikings were approaching.

He watched them as they built and raised trebuchets and catapults, along with drawbridges to lay over the moat that surrounded the stronghold.

Fear started to grow within the Ortaks ranks, as the day went by without any attack. Those men out there seemed to know exactly what to do.

Commander Orthar gave his men orders to place the trebuchets and catapults in the right angle for defence, then he walked amongst his men, to give them orders and to bolster their courage. Many of them had been with the army for many years, but always in the attacking force.

Defending, while locked inside a small space, was not where their strongest tactics lay. They knew that, and they now found themselves in a situation their enemies had always been in.

Oskar knew he had to prepare his army well, if he was to defeat the Ortaks. Their reputation of cruelty in battle and warfare had been described to him on his way, and the information had convinced him of the need to prepare his men properly.

The people they had met on their walk from their homes into Salmon Fjord had told him what kind of an army he was up against. Knowing their strength, he was not going to meet them on an open field.

Hence, he walked straight at them with his army, driving them into a position of defence in their own stronghold. There, he had them just where he wanted them.

His men had built siege machine parts before they headed off to the valley, then they carried them along, or dragged them on wagons; when they reached the valley, they only had to assemble them.

After giving his men orders to assemble the siege machines, he had them bring the fat and the oil that they had gathered in the villages on their way to the valley.

By the evening they were almost finished with their preparation, so he ordered half of his men to stand guard and half of his men to rest. At the crack of dawn, they had finished their work. Then they waited for his orders.

He walked amongst them, setting the courage for the battle ahead, and by midday, he finally reached his post, where he had a good overview of the battlefield. Then he raised his hand.

As one, the Vikings drew the trebuchets closer to the stronghold's wall, and lit the stones covered with fat and oil. Then, by his signal, as one, all the trebuchets released their missiles at the stronghold at the same time.

The Ortaks answered by releasing their own missiles from their war machines, followed by a hail of arrows, but most of the Vikings stood out of reach, waiting for the effect from their own attack.

Again, the Vikings filled their war machines with burning missiles, and again, they released them upon the Ortaks, this time breaking more of the wooden wall than the first round had.

And again, the Ortaks returned a hail of arrows, but the broad Viking shields protected them from the attack.

Now the catapults were drawn into the field, with smaller flaming stones reaching over the walls. Their houses began to burn.

Commander Orthar watched from his tower as the

Vikings organised their attack, and he gave his men orders to prepare themselves for their defence.

He placed them by the wall in four rows, so they were able to shoot the attacking army in a seemingly never-ending hail of arrows. Then he placed his best archers up on the wall, where they could get better aim. He saw the Vikings, as they dragged their trebuchets into the field. Then, suddenly, his stronghold trembled as the flaming missiles crashed against the high wooden wall.

He gave his men who stood with the war machines an order, and they launched their missiles at the Vikings, and then the archers sent their arrows as well, but the Vikings had raised their shields, covering those who were operating their war machines and limiting the damage to almost nothing. He frowned. They were more careful than he had expected.

Only a few moments later, the Vikings launched another attack from the trebuchets, and he saw the wall being smashed to pieces from the heavy stones.

He gave another order, and his men sent another group of arrows over the wall with little result. Then he saw where the Vikings had dragged their catapults onto the field, and the smaller, but more effective missiles started to hit them, reaching into the stronghold and landing on the houses. He gave his men an order to shoot at will, while, at the same time, some of them tried to put out the fires.

For a brief moment Captain Orthar watched his stronghold being burned, but as he turned to take a look at the Vikings, a large rock came down on his watchtower, and in one blow, the flaming missile killed him and smashed the tower to pieces. A few hours later, the whole stronghold was in flames, with black smoke rising up from the fires, blocking the view for those inside it. The Ortaks, choking from the thick smoke and battling for air, did all they could to put out the fires, but there was no recovering from the attack of the Vikings.

That is when Oskar gave his order, and the Vikings who had been waiting out of reach, now ran into the field by the thousands.

They took their stand, and raised their bows. As one they released their arrows into the thick, black smoke rising up from the Ortaks stronghold.

As the smoke covered the view over the fields, a hail of ten thousand arrows came raining down on the Ortaks from all directions. The Ortaks were not prepared for that kind of an attack, and were caught completely unawares.

They either died, or lay wounded by the hundreds, and then another storm of arrows hit them, with the same effect, and even more perished.

Then Oskar gave his final order, as he drew his axe, and by the thousands, as the Vikings lay their drawbridges over the moat, they ran across and into the Ortaks' stronghold.

The Ortaks were a professional and well-organised army, but even such an army has its breaking point. And in the smoke and the confusion, with the arrows raining down on them and the flaming missiles coming, hitting the wall with all their might, shattering it into thousands of pieces, their fighting spirit was extinguished. Then the Vikings came running through the broken wooden wall, from all directions.

Big, wild, and fearful in their ragged, furry clothes, killing everything they saw that stood in their way, the Vikings ran all the way into the middle of the stronghold, where they met confused and frightened men. The Vikings left no man alive that day. By nightfall they finally raised their weapons and shouted in their victory.

Oskar stood there in the middle of the stronghold, holding his bloody war axe over a pile of dead Ortaks, and he turned as he looked around, shouting to his men.

"Burn the rest of the stronghold and those corpses to ashes. I don't want anyone to see that there were ever Ortaks here."

His men followed his orders, but not before they had taken things that were useful, like weapons and armour. And then they raided the stronghold of all valuables.

While his men were at work, he walked up into the valley, and then into the pastures. There were cattle and horses in large numbers pasturing, all the way up the cliffs in the end of the valley. He turned, and as he sat down in the grass to rest for a while, he thought he saw some movements on the other side of the valley. He watched the area for a while. *Must be scouts,* he thought, and stood up again.

There was no need to be worried about scouts, as they would bring the news to their king, making him think twice before sending an army against them.

Two days later the Vikings had gathered the Ortaks live-stock in the valley, along with two hundred horses, and they headed back home.

3 THE BOAR

$\mathcal{I}$t was not until the end of the day that Geirny finally sat down to rest. Behind her was Kings Lake, and she had followed the directions given by the two men who were mending their nets in the village by the lake. Her walk had taken her into a valley, leading toward the mountain pass, and that is where she was heading now.

She had passed a few small villages and farms on her way, where she was told that her father-in-law and his men had passed through two days earlier, and when they heard she was going after him, they gave her some food for her journey.

A young woman gave her a woollen blanket to cover herself with during the cold nights, and she was grateful for her kindness. She wore the blanket across her shoulders, and it gave adequate protection from the increasing cold coming down from the mountains.

That evening she found herself a good campsite over-looking the valley she had just walked through, and she sat there, warming herself by the fire, admiring the view, as her thoughts dwelt on her children. *Where are they now? Are they safe?* The grief was overwhelming, blocking all other thoughts, as she placed her hand over her stomach and began to sob.

After a long, hard cry, she finally managed to lie down and cover her shoulders with her blanket and fall asleep.

She was awakened by a squirrel running across her midriff, followed by a cat. Shocked awake, she immediately jumped to her feet, screaming.

After recovering from that unpleasant experience, she had some breakfast before she headed off again. In front of her were the steep slopes that led up the canyon and all the way into the mountain pass.

The loose gravel made it hard to stay on her feet at times, and she had to be cautious with each step, careful not to fall and hurt herself. Slowly and steadily, though, she went higher and higher up the slope. At noon she stopped to catch her breath, and to look up. She saw that she had made it more than halfway to the top, or so she thought.

They can't have gone this way. Wounded men could not have walked this slope, she thought, as she looked around. Then she saw a path that lay up the slope about two hundred metres on her right. She realised that she had taken a wrong path up the hillside, making it more difficult on herself than was necessary.

Cursing herself for her stupidity, she decided to keep herself on the track she had already taken and continue to the top. Finally, about an hour later, she came across the path that her father-in-law had likely taken, and by the look of all the tracks, many had passed through not so long ago.

She turned to looked back. Down below her feet lay the

beautiful lands of Antonia. Kings Lake, the villages in the valley she had walked, and the farms all lay before her.

Fishing boats were sailing on the clear lake. This seemed so surreal because of what she had gone through. It felt as if the world itself should have stopped, just as hers had. She could see all the way to the woods, where she had killed her attacker, and farther on.

She saw where she had taken the wrong path down in the valley, instead of taking the path that her father-in-law had followed, which led him and his men up into the mountain pass. And again she cursed herself for the mistake. *I could have killed myself. I'm so stupid,* she thought, then she smiled.

After catching her breath and standing there for a while admiring the view, she continued her journey. Ahead lay the mountain pass, and now she took the path that lay through it. By that evening she needed to rest, and she chose a place to lie down by a large rock that would shelter her from the cold breeze. She woke up the next morning cold and stiff, but grateful for the protection. The first snow of winter had lain a white carpet over the landscape. And after dusting the snow off her blanket, she sat up to have some breakfast.

It took a while for the stiffness in her joints to ease, but as the sun made its way through the clouds, and the temperature rose, she grew more and more comfortable. By midday, she had forgotten how cold she had been that morning. The path took her to a river crossing, where the men who had crossed there earlier had left a rope. It had most likely been used for safe crossing with the wounded. She was glad they had left it. She would have had a hard time crossing the river without it. She stopped on the riverbank and watched the strong current for a while.

Even though they had left the safety line, the river was still ice-cold, and she would get soaking wet crossing it. This was not a good thing, but she would press on. She took a deep breath, her heart starting to pound with fear, then she pulled herself together and started making her way across the river.

The shoes given to her by the woman in the village by the lake did not keep her feet dry against the water. The ice-cold water reached her ankles as soon as she stepped forward. After only a few steps the water had reached her thighs, and a few steps more had the water reaching her waist. Now the current was hammering on her from the right, pushing her against the rope.

She was halfway through, the depth of the river had increased, and now it was almost up to her chest, when she felt the rope suddenly go slack. She was terrified that the rope had untied itself on the other side of the riverbank.

Why did I not check the rope before crossing the darn river? she thought. The rope gave in, more and more, as she went farther over the river, but by then, she knew there was no turning back. She had to make it to the other bank or drown.

She managed to make a few more steps in the ice-cold water, though she was shivering violently, and her teeth were chattering loudly in a way she had no control over. The other bank was now getting closer and closer, as she put one foot in front of the other, trying not to let herself float. The bottom of the river was full of large rocks, making it hard to gain a footing. Then, all of a sudden, she felt the rope on the other end beginning to give in too.

She was terrified, her hands and feet were almost numb from the cold, and she was starting to lose the feeling in her feet. Her limbs were turning white, and she was so cold that she was beginning to see stars, finding it hard to keep conscious.

Then she began to feel that she was stepping up in the water again, as she came closer and closer to the other bank. Still holding onto the rope, she somehow made her way up on the riverbank, half crawling by now.

Despite how cold she was, she realised that she had to dry her clothes and warm herself up, if she was not to die from that cold. With her clothes dripping, soaking wet, half-freezing as she moved, she gathered firewood from the wood close by. She stacked it by a rock at the edge of the woodland. She found some shelter from the drafty wind blowing through the canyon under the rock, and she started a fire.

For a while she just sat there, feeling the heat from the fire as it warmed her hands, then she took off her shoes, and warmed her feet. Soon she took off her clothes and placed them on the rock to dry. For the remainder of that day and all the night, she kept her fire going to stay warm and to dry her cloths well enough for her to put them on again, so she could continue her journey.

By morning, she was ready. She took the rope and placed it over her shoulders. *You never know when you may need a rope,* she thought, smiling, pleased with her forethought.

Her pants had shrunk a bit and were fitting her better now, and so was the shirt. In a good mood, she walked the path toward Great Cape.

That evening, after crossing three smaller streams where she only got her feet wet up to her ankles, she finally made it to the edge of the canyon on the other side of the mountain, this time overlooking the valleys of Great Cape. She had crossed King Mountains on her own. She was glad. The worst was over, now to find Captain Kristvar. *He is down there somewhere,* she thought.

She decided to take the path and go farther downhill, before making camp, even though she was tired, having had no sleep the night before.

Carefully, she made her way on the path down the mountainside, and by the time she reached a small, flat pasture that seemed to have been used as a camping place before, it was almost dark. She barely had time to light a fire before the sun had disappeared completely from the sky.

She found herself a soft and good place by the fire, and as soon as she closed her eyes, she fell into a deep sleep.

The walk down from the pass the next morning was light on the feet, and she was optimistic as she reached the woodland below. From what she had seen from up above, looking over the landscape the evening before, she had noticed smoke rising in the air a few kilometres in the direction she was now heading. Maybe it was her father-in-law, or maybe a farm, where she could get some food. She had finished the last of the food she had been given in Antonia the day before.

After about an hour's walk following the path through the woods, she became thirsty, so, hearing water dripping from a small waterfall on the right, she decided to turn off the path and get a drink.

A few steps from the path she entered a clearing. There was a pond there, and to her right, there was a small waterfall. It was a beautiful sight, and she smiled as she stepped into the clearing.

She didn't notice anything amiss at first, but suddenly she heard a sound, coming from the other side of the clearing. And out of the bushes beside the waterfall on her right side, something came running toward her at a great speed—a big, black Boar!

Without a second thought, she started running. She ran so fast that even she had never had any idea that she could move with such speed.

She went through the woods as fast as her feet could possibly carry her, jumping over bushes and streams, hearing the Boar growling and making sounds behind her. She had never heard such sounds before.

She could hear the Boar gaining on her. She ran onto the path again, and after a few moments, she darted to her left, off of the path, and she charged up the steep slope as fast as she could. The slope was covered with last winter's leaves, and as she tried to run up, she found herself struggling for footing as she used her hands and feet to scramble up the slippery slope.

The Boar chased after her, and as she reached the top, she ran across a small stream. Hearing the Boar closing in, she thought she could smell it, it was so close. She saw some rocks on her right side, and ran toward them as fast as she could, but by now, her lungs felt like they were about to burst, and she knew her feet could not carry her much farther. Suddenly, she found herself on an edge of a cliff.

With the Boar only two metres behind her, she jumped from the edge of that cliff with barely a hesitation, not knowing how far below her the ground lay, sure of only one thing: she had to escape the Boar.

Below her was a canyon, and at the bottom sat a big oak, where she landed, amid all the leaves and branches of that big tree. The rope she had slung across her shoulder prevented her from falling to her death. It caught on a big branch as she fell, and swung her around and into the big trunk.

The blow from that impact was so hard, she lost consciousness for a while.

She had no idea how long she hung there in that tree, but when she woke up, she could hear the Boar in the bushes, not far from her. Her chest felt like it was on fire, the pain from the rope bringing tears to her eyes, and she felt blood running down the side of her face. Smashing into the tree face-first had come with consequences, and her left knee was throbbing. Gritting her teeth against the pain, she managed to grab the branch she was hanging from and climb her way up until she could sit on it, leaning against the trunk with a bit of relief.

Sitting there, she tried to gather her thoughts of where she was, and how she could find the path again, if she was able to climb down. But with the Boar still beneath the tree, she was stuck. For now, all she could do was sit and wait and hope the beast would go away.

Nothing like that happened that day. She could hear the beast in the bushes until dark. Unable to sleep, she sat there waiting the whole night. She almost fell asleep once and nearly fell, but her inner thoughts woke her up. Eventually, she stopped hearing the Boar.

Maybe the beast is sleeping, or has it gone away? She kept listening for hours, straining her ears to pick up any sound, but she heard nothing. She saw the daylight begin to remove the darkness, and she was able to see the surrounding area again.

Now is a good time to get down, she thought as she looked at the ground below her. She sighed. It was a long way down, and the pain in her shoulder and breast was even worse than it had been the night before.

She took the rope and tied it around the branch, then she lowered it, carefully, leery that the Boar might still be hanging about in the bushes. But there was no sign of the angry creature.

She sat there listening to the sounds of the woods just in case. She was still scared, but she needed to get down and continue her journey. So, she pulled herself together, and started climbing down the tree, lowering herself on the rope.

She felt a tremendous pain in her chest and shoulder, and she struggled to keep a hold of the rope as she hung there; eventually, she lost her grip and fell down to the ground. Her legs gave out, and she fell on her back, knocking a loud moan from her when she landed.

She lay there for a while perfectly still, listening, terrified and hurt. There was still no sign of the Boar, so she stumbled to her feet again, dusted the leaves and the mud from her clothing, then she started walking in the direction she thought would lead her back to the path.

After half an hour, she came to a small pond and was flooded with relief. She discovered how thirsty she was, and after carefully looking around, convincing herself that she was in no danger, she guzzled the fresh water from the pond.

She felt so much better after that, as if she could now proceed with her task of finding her father-in-law. So she headed off again, and within an hour, she found the path again. She was still scared of running into the Boar, but by the evening she was more and more convinced that she was safe from that beast.

She started looking around for a good place to camp for the night, when she smelled a fire and meat cooking.

Remembering the man in the woods in Antonia, it gave her a fright.

She stopped and looked around, to see if someone was watching her, then she took a turn off the path and into the woods.

Hunger and the need for human interaction were stronger than her fear, so she decided to sneak up on whomever was camping close by.

First she neither saw nor heard anything, but the smell of the campfire and the food was getting stronger, the farther she went.

Then she thought she heard someone talking, and laughing. Her heart rate increased as she went down on all fours, sneaking carefully closer to the camp ahead.

She stopped behind a small bush and carefully peeked between the branches. There were five men and two women by a fire, and what seemed to be a big Boar by their side. The women were skinning it, and they had already placed a good chunk of meat over the fire.

They have killed the Boar! she thought, smiling. She kept herself hidden for a while, thinking about what to do. Those people were not farmers, nor were they soldiers, and hunters they were not. Their clothes were made up of skin and some torn pants and jackets. They looked like they had not taken any kind of bath in years. They were outlaws!

She carefully started to back off, seeking shelter behind a big tree, when she saw one of the men suddenly stand up and look in her direction.

She stopped, and slowly lay herself down on her stomach, not taking her eyes off the man. He gazed into the woods, looking around. This went on for a while, then one of the men handed him a big slice of the meat. He took the offered treat, smiling, and sat down again to eat his meal.

Geirny was so scared at this point that she nearly peed herself. She didn't dare move for a long time, but then it became dark, and she carefully raised herself up on all fours and started to back off again.

She reached the tree, and rolled herself behind it, without making any noise. Stifling the urge to cry out at the pain she still felt was a challenge, but she knew she needed to get around the outlaws and back on the path again. She slowly stood up, and this time she gave the outlaws' camp a wide berth.

Walking through the woods in the dark, without making one noise, is not an easy task, and it took her no less than four hours to circle around them and find the path again. Once she was back on the path and far enough away, she was able to pick up more speed, and, grateful for the moon-light to guide her, she almost ran. She needed to put as much distance between herself and the outlaws as she possibly could.

She kept on until daybreak, then she felt her energy was draining away. She hadn't eaten or slept for too long. Her mind was giving in on her. She knew she needed some rest, and some nourishment if she was to keep on. She looked around and saw a grassy spot not far from the path.

She took a turn off the path and found herself in a grassy clearing. She sat down, immediately feeling the exhaustion taking over. She decided to take a small nap, before heading off again.

She fell asleep as soon as she closed her eyes.

"Look at that, who have we here?" She woke up startled and confused. She sat up, frightened. Two men were standing over her, looking down at her. "Who are you?" one of the men asked, spitting on the ground beside her. She took a better look at the men and saw that they were not the ones she had seen last evening by the fire. These men were wearing uniforms—they were soldiers.

"My name is Geirny." She tried to stand up, but was too tired and in too much pain.

"Here, let me help you." The spitter grabbed her arm, and again she tried to stand, and this time, with his help, it worked. She brushed the grass off her pants, taking a second look at the men.

"Who are you?" she asked. She recognised the uniforms now. "You don't by any chance belong to the group of soldiers who crossed the pass from Antonia?" She felt her heart beating faster in her chest, and she had a hard time containing herself.

"We are, but why do you ask?" The latter looked at her questioningly.

"I am Geirny, Captain Kristvar's daughter-in-law," she said, hardly able to contain her emotions.

They looked at each other. "Then you should come with us," said the spitter, still a bit doubtful. "Don't take this the wrong way, but you do not look so good, my dear," he added.

She did not reply to his comment, but she did try to fix her hair a bit, and brushed down her clothes, with her shivering hands.

"Have you had anything to eat?"

She just shook her head, looking down at the ground, overwhelmed with the attention and the relief she was experiencing.

"Then you should have some of this," the spitter said,

reaching his hand into a small sack that he was carrying, and pulling out a small piece of bread. He handed it to her.

She took the bread, murmuring her thanks before she stuffed it in her mouth. It tasted like heaven. His comrade handed her a skin bottle, full of water, and she ate and drank, standing between them..

"Where is Captain Kristvar?" she asked once she had finished.

"He is at the camp farther in the valley. We will take you there, before we continue hunting," said the spitter, smiling at her.

She took a better look at the men. They were about her age, handsome and well armed, with swords, knives, and bows and arrows.

"I came across a group of outlaws last night," she told them as she pointed in the direction of the outlaws' camp. "There were seven of them," she added. They looked at each other.

"Come now, our horses are down there." The spitter took her by the hand. It was a short walk, and they helped her up on one of the horses, then they walked down the path, leading the horses. One hour later they came to a small, grassy valley, where they had made their home after the passing.

Captain Kristvar was standing outside his hut when they approached. They took her all the way, and stopped in front of him. They did not say a word. At first he did not recognise her. But as she dismounted, with help from the spitter, and she stood there right in front of him, a smile that spread across his face told her that he knew who she was.

~

FIVE MONTHS HAD PASSED since Caleb arrived as a commander in the royal army of Montania at Rutan City. He had used that time well. He had organised an intelligence network, to investigate who of those noblemen and locals had helped the Ortaks to invade the city and Montania, without any resistance.

He wanted to find them all, and he was in no hurry. His boss had been granted lordship and given the castle at Rutan, along with the city and the surrounding area. Everything that had belonged to his predecessor, Lord Gerwald, was now his.

At the end of the search, his intelligence officers had made a long list of men, and women, who had helped the Ortaks invade the city. They were further engaged in hunting down people, men, women, and children, whom the Ortaks had captured and shipped out as slaves to Orknia.

He had made it clear to his men that they were to do nothing to startle the traitors, but to make them feel safe in their homes. Time for revenge would come later.

It came as a surprise to him, how many people the Ortaks had bribed prior to their invasion, to make sure that everything went smoothly after they had landed at Rutan Harbour.

He also heard that many of the traitors had fled into the woods, or crossed the Great River, either to Eniktronia or Antonia. They had decided to escape the wrath of the people, who had lost their loved ones as a result of the traitors' selfishness.

Then he laid out his plan to his officers and divided them into groups, giving them assignments to see to.

The plan was simple. They had all the names and whereabouts of the traitors. The troops would go to their posts and wait until sunset. Then, as one, they would attack. His message was clear: no traitor was to be left alive!

He waited at the castle, and just before sunset, he walked out to the balcony and listened to the sound of the city. There were a few wagons on the move, other than that, all was peaceful and quiet. Then a whistle was heard, then another one, until more than twenty whistles sounded across the city, as a signal to his soldiers to storm into the houses of the traitors, and carry out the orders he had given them. Then all went quiet again. Moments later, he heard the footsteps of his soldiers, as they marched through the streets, and out of the city, dragging wagons with the corpses of the traitors, to be buried outside the city.

He waited until he heard them no more, then he stepped inside again. He was not happy. Sad and quiet, he walked to a table in the main hall, where he poured himself a cup of water and drank it all.

He heard footsteps in the castle corridor, and a moment later, the commander of the castle guard entered the hall, informing him that everything had been performed as planned.

He did not reply, but nodded and sat down in the chair at the end of the table.

And once more, his thoughts were of the family he once had.

4 THE AMBUSH

*P*rincess Tania and Prince Storgard had been waiting for a report from Ylfa and Arthenth at the gap for some time now. And to keep themselves busy, they trained hard, keeping themselves in good shape.

Tania's men had raised her a large house on a hill nearby, and she enjoyed the view over the Elven and the Barbarian campsite. At this moment there were twenty-thousand soldiers in the camp. They were waiting for the order to engage the enemy from the Underworld and to defend the wall surrounding the great gap.

Messengers and scouts were also arriving daily from the outposts of Alfheim, informing her that all was quiet and peaceful. They seemed to have eliminated the threat from the Underworld for now.

But experience had taught the Elves not to brag at triumph. There would always be evil to fight. So they sent out patrols and kept their eyes out for the enemy.

One afternoon, the horn at the wall blocking the great

gap sounded out loud. A few minutes later, two messengers, one from each tribe, entered Alfheim through the gap.

Tania watched from her balcony as they entered the camp through the wall's gate, moving into the campsite, where they met up with Prince Storgard. Then they took the road leading up to her house, as they walked along with the commanding officers of both armies, the Elven and the Barbarians. Prince Storgard took the lead, and it was obvious by the look of them that they had news.

On the ground floor of her house was a meeting hall for the army council, and Tania was quite excited when she walked into the hall and took her seat down at the end.

A few minutes later, Prince Storgard entered the hall, and in slow, measured steps, he took his place beside her. He bowed his head a little, then turned, facing the door. Tania gave her guard a signal to let the others inside. They entered one by one and bowed for the princess and the prince.

"We have been waiting for news from the cave. What do you have for us?" Tania said, looking at the messengers. She had a hard time hiding her excitement.

The messengers reached into their bags for the reports and handed them to their masters. They were quiet while reading, then the messengers answered all her questions. After that, Tania turned her speech to Prince Storgard.

"It looks like our mission has been successful, but what do we do now? Do we wait to see what happens, or do we go down there with our armies and attack that city in the Underworld in hopes we can eliminate the threat once and for all?"

"I say we go down there. Waiting will only give our enemy the chance to reunite and attack us again," he replied convincingly.

"You are probably right. We should go down there and regain those lands, and bring light into this world again," she said as if to herself, lost in deep thought. She then turned to her commanding officers.

"Send out an order for the army to be assembled, and have them all here in the valley within ten days from now. We will enter the cave and free our lands from this evil once we are ready." They bowed and left to follow her orders.

"I will send out a request for reinforcement to my king, but it will take longer than ten days," said Prince Storgard. Princess Tania nodded, smiling.

Finally, things are looking better, if we can reunite with the Barbarian army, then we do stand a chance of defeating in this war and can put an end to this once and for all, she thought as she watched Prince Storgard leave to send his report and request.

She patted her wolf, Tyr, on his head and gave the guard an order to have her horse readied. She could not wait any longer to see the cave and what was in it for herself.

She rode down into the camp, which was turning into a town of Barbarians and Elves, and made her way to Prince Storgard's house.

She dismounted and went inside, just as he was finishing with his report. He handed his report to his messenger, looking surprised at the sight of Tania in the doorway.

"What brings you here so soon?" he asked as he gestured at the messenger to leave, nodding his head in the direction of the door.

"The Cave. I can't wait any longer to see what we are facing. I would like to evaluate the circumstances for myself," she said firmly.

He stood there, thinking, for a while before he nodded.

"I will go with you. They might need reinforcement down there, so we should bring them some more men," he replied. "Give me one hour to assemble the troops," he added.

"All right, then. We leave in one hour," she said, smiling with excitement.

One hour later, they headed off through the gap, the gap that she had stopped the Elven sorceress from closing completely.

They went onto the path that took them through Black Woods, to the cave. Along with fifty of her men, she decided to go on foot, this first trip but kept Tyr at her side. Tyr could smell trouble a mile away. Besides, he would not have been happy if she left him behind.

They went inside the cave, and just as their scouts had informed them, the smell was strong. Elven light had been placed on torches that were on the walls, so it was as bright as daytime inside the cave.

With Prince Storgard at her side, Tania followed the messengers through the cave, and all the way to the staircase, leading them down into the world where Ylfa and Arthenth waited for them.

Halfway down the stairs, she stopped.

She was astonished when she looked over the landscape, remembering that the report from Arthenth and Ylfa said these lands once were part of Alfheim. She could hardly believe that the Elves had no knowledge of this, though she had never heard anyone speaking about it.

Then she heard a low drumming sound in the distance, and some mixed and strange feelings rose up in her as she was standing there. She turned to Prince Storgard. He remained beside her on the staircase.

"Did you know of this world?"

"No, I did not, but there must be some knowledge or documents in the world of Alfheim, or in our lands," he replied, without taking his eyes off the landscape.

"Exactly what I was thinking," she said quietly.

"That is where we left them. They are waiting for us down there," the Elven messenger interrupted their thoughts to say, as he pointed to the right. Some distance from the staircase they saw ruins up on a hill.

"Well, then, show us the way there, and we will follow," Tania replied, smiling.

As they stepped down on the floor of that world, Tania felt it tremble slightly under her feet from the drums in the distance. They crossed the terrain carefully, ready if they were attacked.

Two hours later, they entered the ruins, where Arthenth and Ylfa greeted their masters and royalty.

Tania was glad to see them alive and safe in the horrible place, but then she walked over to Trinserant. He was sitting calmly and smiling when she and Storgard approached him, but he was still bound by his feet, and two men were guarding him at all times, so he could not escape.

"I have read the report and seen your lands here. Is there anything else you want to add to what you have already said?" Tania looked at Trinserant carefully as he tried standing up, but the rope around his feet was getting in his way.

"No, Your Highness, not that I can think of." He fell backwards, landing on his behind.

"Loosen up those ropes," she ordered the guards.

"We have heard about Gruntentorg, the city of Dark

Elves, but what can you tell us about those drums?" asked Prince Storgard, standing beside Tania.

"Those are the war drums of Ekaner. The Ekaner Guards beat them endlessly," he replied, while he raised himself up again.

"War drums of Ekaner? Ekaner Guards?" Tania repeated. "Do we have to be worried about them?" She looked worried.

"No, Your Highness, not when you hear them. Only if you do not hear them," he replied.

"What will happen then?" Prince Storgard frowned.

"Well, last time, and the only time since I have been here, that those drums stopped, the Underworld Army emerged, and marched through these lands and passed here as they entered the world of Alfheim—you know the rest," Trinserant looked at them, and he was a bit frightened.

"Who are those Ekaner Guards?" asked Tania.

"Well, I have never seen them, but from what I have been told, they are huge trolls, and they are the guards and door-keepers to the Underworld, or Ekaner, as the Dark Elves call it," replied Trinserant, with a shiver in his voice.

"Where is the gap into the Underworld?" asked Prince Storgard.

"I have never seen that, either. It is way beyond Grunten-torg, at least six days' journey from the city, perhaps more," he replied, and unconsciously, Tania and Storgard looked in the direction of the city.

Tania and Storgard stood there, looking over the land-scape, silent for a while as they each thought over what they had learned. This is a terrible place to be, and he has been here for decades, poor man, thought Tania. However, she sensed that he was not telling them everything he knew, and she wanted to know more before sending the whole Elven Army into these lands.

"You claim that there are many small towns and villages beyond those mountains over there." She pointed in the direction of the mountains on their left side.

"Yes." He nodded and looked to the mountains, but she saw something in his eyes before he quickly looked down again.

"What is it that you are not telling us? There is something else on the other side of those mountains, isn't there?" She was becoming impatient and angry.

"There is a castle and another city, not as big as Gruntentorg though, it does not have as many Dark Elves, but it has many slaves.

"And then there is a lake." He paused. "Beyond the lake, there is the old gap into Alfheim." He was obviously scared and dared not look up.

"What do you mean the old gap into Alfheim? What lake?" Tania was getting angrier.

"That gap has been closed for a very long time, but as I have told the others, this was a part of Alfheim once." He was still afraid to look up.

"Have you seen this gap?" Tania was starting to get a bit worried now. What if there is another way into Alfheim, and the Underworld Army can enter there?

"No, Your Highness, it was closed a long, long time ago, long before my time." He shook his head.

"Do you know where it opens to in Alfheim?"

"Yes, it opens in a valley one day west from Elvengard. At the end of that valley, there is a small stream coming down the hillside, forming a beautiful waterfall as it goes off a small cliff. Beside that waterfall is a grassy pasture slope.

That is where the gap was." He now looked up, convinced that he was not in more trouble with the royalty.

"How do you know this?" Tania lifted her eyebrows.

"I was shown the opening as a young man before I came down here, and I saw a scripture about it in a scroll, along with the magic words that must be said for one to open the gate," he replied.

"Do you remember the words?" asked Prince Storgard in a sceptical manner.

"No, my lord, I do not. Like I said, I was young. It was a long time ago."

"What else can you tell us about that lake?"

"Not much. It is a big lake, and the city and the castle are by the lake. Why?" He looked surprised by all the questions about the lake.

"We just wanted to know how to get across," she said and frowned.

"You just get around it to the gap," he replied. "Well, it will take you three days, but then you don't have to cross it on a boat." He looked at them, still confused.

Tania gave Prince Storgard a sign to follow her, to talk in private.

"If we summon our armies down here, how soon do you think the Dark Elves will find out?" asked Tania, looking at Storgard.

"Hard to say, but from what he has told our men, they usually send someone around here every now and then, and there has been no one since the Underworld Army passed here. If we were to bring our entire army down here, they would probably know about that within a few days, at most," said Prince Storgard.

"He claims it is a five-day journey to Gruntentorg, and

that would give them enough time to prepare to defend the city," Tania said, looking at Prince Storgard. He nodded.

"There is also that matter with the other gap. If there is a scroll with the magic words to open that gap, we should find it and do so, for two reasons. This world needs sunshine in it, and the other reason, is that we can enter this world much faster with an opening directly from Alfheim," said Tania, and turned her head, looking over the terrain.

"I agree. We should return and wait for our army, and prepare for that warfare, but we need to find the scroll. Maybe there is one, either at the Elven or Barbarian archives. Our king should be informed of this as well," replied Prince Storgard.

"I agree. Let's return to Alfheim. Maybe our kings will know something we don't," said Tania, then she turned to Arthenth.

"We will leave those who came down here with us under your command, and you will wait here for further orders," she commanded. He bowed before his princess.

An hour later Princess Tania and Prince Storgard returned the way they came with ten of their personal guards each.

Arthenth and Ylfa watched them as they left, climbing up the stairs before entering the cave.

"Your royalty should have more protection going into that cave," they heard Trinserant call at them from where he sat. They looked at each other.

"What is he talking about?" Ylfa looked at Arthenth in surprise.

"There could be Demons in there, a lot of Demons," he called at them again.

"There were no Demons in there when we came

through, nor when they came through," said Ylfa as she ran toward Trinserant.

"You may not have seen any, but that does not mean that they aren't there. There are many secret doors they could be hiding behind," he said convincingly.

She looked at Arthenth, frightened.

"Guard him well," he ordered the men they had put in charge of the strange old man. "The rest of you, come with me," he added in a commanding and loud voice.

Ylfa lifted her hand and called out a war cry to her men, who came running after her as she rushed over the terrain beside Arthenth, toward the staircase and the cave.

They were so frightened for their royalties' lives that they did not speak a word. They just ran as fast as they could.

PRINCESS TANIA and Prince Storgard entered the hall by the top of the staircase. As they entered the cave, Tania stopped to take a better look around the hall.

She was not tired, she was in an excellent physical form, and lifelong training had taught her to pick a pace suitable for travelling a distance, so she did not need to rest, but her curiosity had to be satisfied.

The information she had gotten from Trinserant had raised more questions that needed to be answered.

The hall had been lit up by Elven light on the stone pillars that were holding up the ceiling by the time Arthenth and Ylfa crossed the hall, casting a view to the staircase where they now stood. It made a well-lit path, for those who passed through the cave.

"It looks to me that this part of the cave is much older

than the tunnel at the other end, by Black Wood," she said in a low voice, looking around inside the hall.

"You might be right, and it could even have been here at the time the world we just came from was a part of Alfheim," replied Storgard.

She nodded in silence and started walking to the right, Tyr following her wherever she went. After she had taken a few steps, however, the wolf began to growl. Then she knew they were not alone.

She stopped and looked at Storgard, and they drew their swords simultaneously, as did their guards who had been in their company since they headed back from the ruins.

They all stood there perfectly still. Then they heard a noise coming from a dark corner, where the light did not reach. They stood there, straining to see into the shadows, but they heard nothing. There was no more sound, all was quiet, but when she laid her hand on Tyr's head, she noticed that he was shivering.

She nodded her head to one of her guards, and he took a step in front of them. He had a bow in his hand and an arrow at the ready, with a small Elven light ball at the end. He placed his hand on the light ball, and it lit up. Then he raised his bow and shot the arrow into the shadows, where they had heard the sound coming from.

They followed the path of the arrow, all eyes glued to its flight as it went far into the corner of this vast hall. They saw something that gave them a tremendous shock, a large number of big, black Demons, wearing full armour, stood there in the dark, as if they were waiting for someone to give them an order.

The arrow pierced a Demon in front of the group, and the beast cried out at the pain, creating complete chaos amongst the others. Unfortunately, the light was extinguished when the arrow hit the Demon, and the area was once again immersed in blackness. All was quiet for a short moment.

Then they heard a terrible racket and screams as the Demons came running out of the shadows and straight at them. At first, it seemed there were only a few, but they were soon running out into the light in great numbers and from all directions. They must have been waiting in the shadowed corners of the great hall the entire time. The terrifying crowd of bloodthirsty beasts increased rapidly.

When they entered the Elven light, their blindness overtook them, but they ran forward despite it, waving their weapons and screaming with anger, so it echoed in the great hall.

The Demons' lack of sight gave the Elven archers an excellent opportunity to shoot them without any difficulties, and they brought them down as fast as they could draw their bows. Screaming and crying out, the Demons fell by the arrows, but it did not slow them down.

They had no time to rethink their options, and there was nowhere to run. So Tania and Storgard, along with their personal guards, readied themselves for the impact.

With her sword in her right hand and her long hunting knife in her left, Tania defended herself in swift moves, trying to move away from the horrible weapons coming at her, at the same time she chopped them down, one by one.

A huge Demon steamed straight at her with great speed, with his spear aimed at her, but quietly and swiftly she moved out of his way, so he passed her, running into another Demon behind her, coming from the other direction.

Tyr took off into the blinded crowd of Demons, attacking and defeating them one by one. They were utterly defenceless against the wolf's attack, but some of them tried to hit him with their spears, or their axes. He was too swift, and they succeeded only in beating or stabbing each other.

In a huge rage, the Demons continued their attack, as the Elves and Barbarians defended themselves against the bloodthirsty horde. Although blinded, the Demons had surrounded them, waving their weapons and screaming and shouting as they attacked in ever-growing numbers.

If ever Tania was happy about her strict training schedule every morning, and the teaching from Oskar, the monk at the monastery in Big Canyon as a child, it was now.

Using everything she had been taught, and her increasing skills throughout the years, she was able to hold her own in the battle.

As the battle raged on, she had to use every miscue and technique she was capable of. In the heat of all the fighting, she felt her senses and her intuition growing stronger and stronger. Her foreseeing and senses had never been so accurate.

Like always, this was a welcomed battle for the Barbarians, and they chopped the Demons down with their weapons, one by one, as they approached them, taking great pleasure in doing so.

This went on for a long while, where they all managed to defend themselves, but more and more Demons came to fill the place of those they had killed, and they were starting to get tired.

Not a second of rest for anyone, as they had to protect themselves from being stabbed or chopped by an axe, spear, or a sword, and Tania was starting to realise that they had met their destiny in this cave. Too many Demons were coming too fast; they would not be able to stand against them for much longer. But they kept on fighting.

The Elven steel in their weapons and their armour played a significant role in keeping them alive. For more than a thousand years, the Elves had developed steel that was light as a feather, but as sharp as razors, and with this kind of armour, they stood against all the odds. An Elven sword went through the thickest armour from the Underworld, like a knife through butter, while the Elven armour, as thin and light as it was, gave better defence than the thickest steel armour the Demons wore.

As far as Tania knew, Tyr was still someplace in there amongst the Demons, and she hadn't seen or heard him for a while; she did not know if he was alive. She knew the end would be soon. She could tell that both the Elven and the Barbarian guards were tiring out. Many were wounded, and the Demons were just too many. The number of them was overwhelming, their efforts seeming to make no difference, no matter how many they slew.

She cursed and blamed herself when she took a hard blow in the thigh, but the Elven plate armour protected her this time, and she stabbed the Demon in the eye and through his head, at the same time defending herself from a spear coming at her from the other direction.

Then one Elf fighting beside her, fell down with a spear in his shoulder, and almost at the same time, another one took a hit straight on the forehead, and he fell dead on the spot.

So this is the end, then, she thought, as she gave a Demon his death blow, just as he was about to hit Prince Storgard in the back, who was distracted while fighting three other Demons. There seemed to be no end to the reinforcements of the Demons, and they were making no progress.

The battle raged on, and they were losing more of their guards now, whether wounded or killed.

After a while, only five of the Elven guards and six of the Barbarian guards were still standing, and yet, there were no fewer bloodthirsty Demons.

They were trying to step back as the corpses kept piling up around them and under their feet.

And still, they came.

Tania sensed that her muscles were getting sore, and her breath was getting shorter, but she had to keep on with the same speed in defence and attack if she was to stay alive.

It seemed that Prince Storgard still had all his strength and stamina, and she marvelled at his level of fitness. When she looked in his direction, he was cutting a Demon in two with his sword, and blocking an incoming attack from another almost at the same time with his left hand, where he had his armoured sleeve.

They were all covered in blood by now, and as she took a look at the guards, she realised there were now only two of the Elven guards and three of the Barbarian guards left. Suddenly a big wave of Demons hit them, and she realised that she had no more fight in her.

Two more Demons cut down, as she used the last of her energy to behead one with her sword, then stabbed the other one in the heart with her knife. Then she looked up and saw a big black Demon in front of her; he had raised his axe above his head to chop her.

She had no defence for that blow, and she knew well that was the case, but she was so tired, she almost didn't care any more. For a split of a second, she waited for her death.

But the Demon stood still, then she saw the Demon's head being split in two, by a big sword.

It was Prince Storgard, and almost simultaneously an arrow passed her and slammed into a Demon's forehead that was attacking her from her right, followed by a large number of arrows, killing the enemy all around her.

What happened next was something she had not expected. The Demons that had surrounded them were either chopped down or shot by arrows in a great number, and before she had time to think, her men, led by Arthenth, rushed into the battle, killing anyone in their way.

Quickly, she was protected from arrows and spear throws, by a wall of shields held by her own men, and she just stood there and lowered her hands. Then, slowly, she sheathed her sword and knife.

She felt how her hands quivered with fatigue and fear. She looked at them, then she moved her fingers and clenched her fists.

Never had she been so close to death. She had stared death straight in the face this day. She was on the brink of crying, both from exhaustion and relief, but her place as their leader demanded she not give in to her emotions.

She lowered her hands again, and just stood there, staring straight forward with empty eyes, exhausted and frightened when she felt something.

The back of her hand was being licked. Surprised, and with joy, she recognised the feel of that warm tongue—Tyr had returned!

She sank down on the floor and welcomed her friend with a big hug. And like he always did, he licked her face and sat on her lap, like he had been doing since he was a puppy, even though he was much too big for that now.

And by doing so now, she was able to hide her tears from the world, by burying her face in his furry neck. And for a long while, she stayed right there.

Then she pulled herself together, and with every muscle in her body aching, she managed to stand up again, just in time to see her men finishing the last of the Demons.

Prince Storgard had joined his men, to finish this fight. He now approached her as she stood there in the middle of the hall, and he stopped in front of her and nodded his satisfaction.

"It was an honour to fight with you, Princess," he said as he sheathed his great sword.

"It was an honour to fight with you too, Prince Storgard." She smiled, then she frowned. "We must clean out this cave, if there is any chance that more creatures are lurking in here somewhere," she added as she turned to Arthenth and Ylfa, who had just returned from fighting the last of the Demons, and had placed themselves in front of her. "I never thought I would be so happy to see your sorry faces, as I was now. What brought you up here?" She looked at each of them, and she still felt shaken after all the excitement, and the fight for her life.

"Trinserant did, My Princess. He told us that you might be in danger," Arthenth replied.

"Well, I'm glad he did, but you should search for a doorway or some sort of opening within the hall. I am pretty sure there were no Demons in here when we passed through earlier." She looked at Prince Storgard, and he nodded in agreement.

Arthenth bowed and left to carry out her orders, in Ylfa's company.

"We should send for reinforcement. There is no way of

knowing what lies within these walls," said Prince Storgard, as he turned his head to look around.

The Elven light had now been placed in every corner of the hall, or so it seemed, but still, their men were going in large groups farther and farther to each side, and deeper into the hall behind the staircase, like there, was no end to all this.

"Yes, we should," replied Tania in a low voice, while looking around, as the hall was being lit up by her men and the Barbarians. She gave two of her guard the order to head for Alfheim and fetch five hundred men, and bring them here as fast as possible. Prince Storgard gave the same order to his men.

"That should be enough," he said as he frowned. The fight had taken most of his energy, she knew, even though he was too proud to show it.

A few moments later, two of her guard approached with an old wooden bench they had found, and they placed it on the floor beside her. They said nothing, but took two steps back, to give her space. She nodded thankfully for the opportunity to sit and rest for a while.

After she sat down, Prince Storgard hesitated, and she could tell that he would have liked to sit as well. Showing fatigue in front of his men, however, was not an option for a warrior and a leader of the Barbarians.

Tania realised his predicament, so after a short, while sitting on the bench, which was big enough for both of them, she turned her words to the prince as she patted Tyr on the head.

"Sit down here beside me, Prince Storgard. I can't be looking up at you as if I'm a child when I'm talking to you," she said in a demanding voice. For a while, he hesitated, but then he reached for his belt holding his sword, and placed it over his shoulder, with his big sword on his back. He sat down beside her, sitting straight, and looking straight forward.

Keeping one's dignity is one thing, but sitting like there is a stick up his arse in another matter altogether, she thought.

They had only been sitting there for a while when Arthenth and Ylfa returned.

"Our men found a tunnel on the other side of the hall, and we have lined them up against it, in case there are more of those Demons inside. We are waiting for further instructions, My Princess," Arthenth said.

"Why does that not surprise me?" she mumbled. "You reported in your letter to me that you had made sure this passing was safe, Captain." She was angry and frowned heavily.

"Forgive me, Your Highness." He bowed, casting his eyes to the floor. "What are your orders?" he added in a low voice.

"We have sent for reinforcements, and we will wait until they have returned before exploring what is within those tunnels." She was less angry now. "You should keep on looking for more openings into the hall. Those Demons seemed to be coming from all directions," she added.

"Will do, Your Highness." He bowed and left.

Until now Ylfa had not said a word, but now she stepped in front of Prince Storgard.

"Forgive me, my prince. We sent our scouts to search the hall, and we were informed that the hallways were empty." She bowed down to one knee.

He said nothing but nodded his head, and she stood up again, then left to follow the orders along with Arthenth.

"You don't say much, do you?" Tania asked in a low voice.

"I speak when there is something to say," he replied firmly.

Typical man. She sighed.

He acted like he didn't notice.

They had been sitting for only a few moments when they were brought water to drink and some food.

They sat quietly while they enjoyed the water and meat. Tania had always found Elven food to be more energetic than the food in Mannheim.

They had barely finished when an Elven messenger came running into the great hall. Tania looked up when she heard the racket as he entered the hall and was being stopped by the guard. She waited patiently until he approached her. He stopped five metres in front of her and bowed.

"I have a message from the king," he said as he reached inside his jacket and brought out a letter that was sealed with the royal seal.

She opened the letter and read it. Afterwards, she sat there for a while, thinking, as she found her strength returning after the meal.

"This is an order from my father, King Ethan. I am to meet up with him at Elvengards. He seems to know about the lands down from the cave."

"I must return back home, too, to meet up with my king. If we are going to war in another world, I will need more men, and the support from the war council as well," replied Prince Storgard. "I think we should leave it to Ylfa and Arthenth to clear out this cave," he added as he stood up.

"I agree." She patted Tyr on the head, then she joined the prince as he crossed the hall and entered into the tunnel leading to Black Wood, and the world of men. He did not like to enter Mannheim, but that was the only way open to them, to take the path through the wood and back into Alfheim. They had almost made it through the cave when they met the reinforcement they had sent for. As they stepped aside to make room so their men could pass inside the tunnel, each of them saluted their royalty.

It was a relief for them to breathe the air in Mannheim as they stepped outside the cave and into the fresh air of Black Wood. For some reason, the woods seemed greener, or so thought Tania.

Prince Storgard was not at ease until he had entered Alfheim again. This was the air he was used to, and he felt the best while filling his lungs with it.

She bid Prince Storgard farewell and headed for her house upon the hillside. She decided to rest before heading to Elvengards, since it would take her at least three, maybe four, days to make the trip.

Coming to the house, she turned. She sensed that something had changed. She felt how her senses had strengthened, during the fight in the cave, hearing, now and seeing everything more clearly.

She was able to hear Prince Storgard giving his men orders, and she did not only see, but she could also hear when one of the guards rode off.

She looked at Tyr, standing beside her, and it was as he sensed her changes. She patted him on the head and went inside her house.

5 INVADING HERGIA

Commander Triskar of the Ortaks Army had just finished his breakfast in his tent when he was interrupted by one of the guards.

"A guard from the gate has arrived and asks to approach you, Commander," said the guard.

The commander nodded and stood up from the table to put on his armour.

The guard from the gate entered. "There is a messenger from Crystal City, and he asked for permission to see the commander," he said

"Then send him to me," he commanded.

The guard saluted and rushed out of the tent. The commander could hear the sound from his footsteps fading away, as the guard ran in the direction of the gate. The commander stepped outside his tent, to be greeted by his men.

He looked around. The morning air was cold, and a drizzle hit his face as he looked towards the wall. They had been camped by White River for almost a month now, waiting for orders from his general in Crystal City of what steps to take next.

He had five thousand men under his command, and they were getting restless. They were in a foreign country, and they needed to have a task of some sort or something to fight. If they did not have an assignment soon, they would begin fighting amongst themselves.

They had raised a high rampart around the camp and were well prepared for combat.

His scouts had scanned the northern part of Antonia, as far south as Bending Pass, and east all the way to the borders of Great Cape and the King Mountains, so he had a good idea of what to expect from the locals. From what he knew, there was no threat of an attack.

The scouts he had sent into Hergia and Great Cape had informed him of the location of their army troops, and their defences. Everything seemed to be in order; only a few scouting missions from the Duke of Great Cape had been spotted here and there.

He waited patiently in front of his tent, and a few minutes later, the messenger arrived. Actually, there were two of them, and they looked like their journey from the city had been a rough one. Their horses were almost to the point of exhaustion, and their uniforms ragged.

The commander acted as if he didn't notice, but hurried to grab the bag they were carrying, as one of them extended it towards him.

They did not say a word, and neither did the commander. He turned around and went into his tent, and the messengers left in the company of guards. Being weary and hungry, they needed to be fed and take time to rest before they returned to the city with an answer to the general.

Commander Triskar placed the leather bag on the table, then he opened it. Inside was a map of Hergia and a sealed envelope containing his long-awaited orders. He was to bring his troops across the White River and secure a safe passing across for the Ortaks Army. He was to do so by raising a stronghold on the other bank of the river and building a bridge crossing White River. Once that was completed, he was instructed to wait for further orders.

He sat there for a while, with the letter and the map, considering what his next step should be. This was not an easy task. For a commander in the Ortaks Army, failure was not an option. He would be executed, as would his family in Orknia if he failed to complete his task.

First of all, he needed to get his men across the river. According to the information his scouts had given him, and from what his guards could see where they stood up on the wall, he knew that the Hergian Army had raised a stronghold on the opposite side of the river. He could even see their watchtowers from his own wall.

Based on the information his scouts had gathered, he knew they had at least four thousand men-in-arms in that stronghold. Furthermore, they had no less than two thousand soldiers guarding the riverbank, from White Lake in the East to Utanium Mountains in the West, who could be used for reinforcement if they were attacked.

He stood up and went outside again. In deep thought, he walked over to the wall facing the river and Hergia. He walked the steps leading up to the watchtower, and as he entered, his men saluted him, a bit frightened and surprised to see their commander.

He stood there, thinking. The river was both deep and wide. Crossing it would mean a broad, massive floating bridge. That was not a problem. There was plenty of woodland in the area they could use to build that, but as soon as his men started building the floating bridge on the riverbank, the enemy on the opposite bank would strengthen their defences and make sure there were war machines in place, to break that floating bridge down, even as it was still being built. He would lose too many—likely most—of his men trying to get across that way.

He stood in one place for almost an hour, thinking, trying to decide which way to accomplish what he had been commanded to do, without too many casualties.

He had well-trained, professional soldiers; he trusted that they would prevail if he could only get them on the other side of the river without losing too many men. On even ground, they were superior to an inexperienced army like the Hergians.

Then he realised something.

When he started to build a floating bridge here on the riverbank, the enemy would call in all their reinforcements, and prepare for the invasion right here. They would expect him to attack straight across the river. He stood there for a moment, smiling, then he turned and walked down the stairs. As he approached his tent, he addressed one of his guards.

"Get me the messengers," he commanded before he turned to enter his tent.

He took off his armour, and then he wrote his reply to his general. He sealed the letter and put it into the leather bag.

"No one may see this except General Akhtar," he

ordered as he handed the bag to the messengers. They took the bag and saluted, then they left the same way they arrived, moving fast as they rode out of camp.

Commander Triskar sat at his desk, planning his strategy in more detail. He examined the map he had received from his general. It showed detailed information about Hergia; having such an informative source made his strategy easier, and he was grateful for the talent of his scouts.

A few hours later, he called for a meeting with his officers, to lay down his plan for an attack.

It was noon when the last of his officers arrived at his tent. Many of them knew him well. They had been with him for more than a decade and had faced many enemies under his command. They would trust him with their lives.

"We have been given orders to cross the river into Hergia and secure a safe passage for our army," he said in a powerful voice.

"With all due respect, Commander, how are we going to accomplish that? There are at least four thousand Hergian troops on the other side of the river." His old and trusted friend Captain Rolanus had spoken out.

"Diversion! That is how, and from our info, they likely have six thousand soldiers on the other side of the river." Commander Tristan paused and let his men ingest that for a moment. They looked a bit surprised but waited for further information from their commander.

"We will start building a floating bridge that will be used to cross the river here in the future, but for now, it will serve only as a distraction. Meanwhile, we will send four thousand of our troops straight south, taking the road to Crystal City from our camp." He looked at Captain Rolanus. "That group will be led by you." Then he looked and spoke to the others.

"You will leave in small groups. Half a day's walk from here, you will be well out of sight, then you will turn west.

"There is a valley about a day and a half from there. The locals call it Deer Valley. There, the army will wait for four days. That will give the Hergian Army enough time to call in their troops, those who are defending alongside the river-bank, as a reinforcement.

"Our army will use the woodland and the high ridge in the valley for cover. After four days, you will approach the river with your troops, straight north from the valley.

"From there, your troops should be able to cross the river unseen. The Hergian Army will have called for reinforce-ment along the riverside, to their location here, leaving the rest of the riverside defenceless.

"From the reports we have from our scouts, you will find yourself in a remote area. There are neither farms nor villages nearby on the Hergia side of the river." The commander pointed his finger at the map.

"We will keep the Hergian Army occupied here, by building the floating bridge in front of their eyes. They will be expecting us to cross and attack from here." The commander looked up from the map and to his men, the barest hint of a smile curving his lips.

"When you have crossed the river, you will head south for half a day, then turn east until you are straight north from the Hergian stronghold. You will find yourself in a field, where you can stand your ground against the Hergian troops if they attack you.

"The Hergian Army will either attack you with their

army, on the battlefield, or they will retreat into their stronghold.

"Either way, it will allow us to place the floating bridge across the river, and to send you reinforcements.

"I will be stationed here at the camp, while Captain Rolanus will lead the invading army into Hergia.

"That is all, Gentlemen, this meeting is adjourned. Captain Rolanus, you will stay for a moment longer," demanded the commander.

"That is a bold move you have decided on, Commander," said the captain in a low voice.

"Yes, and that is why it must work, Captain." The commander did not look up from the map. He pointed his finger on the spot where he wanted his troops to cross. "You must use the time you have for waiting in the valley to build barges," he said, and one could hear some anxiety in his voice.

"Of course, Commander. You can count on us. We will prevail in this task," said Captain Rolanus convincingly.

The commander nodded. "I know that we will, Captain, but you should go now and prepare for your journey into Hergia. Good luck, Captain," he said. The captain saluted and left the tent.

IT WAS STILL early morning when Kristjan, commander of the royal army of Hergia, stood in one of his stronghold's towers and watched the Ortaks across White River. His men had informed him of some change in the Ortaks behaviour for the last two hours.

"The Ortaks seem to be building some sort of bridge or other," they had said.

It did not take him long to realise that they were building a floating bridge.

They were preparing to invade Hergia!

He ran down the stairs leading up to the tower and called out to his commanding officers who were standing nearby waiting for his orders.

"Call in the patrol groups from the riverbank."

He was not going to let the Ortaks get away with this. He would drown them in the river if they dared try to cross. He was furious.

"How dare they?" He rushed into his quarters and screamed with anger.

He moved over behind the table in the corner, thinking. Five of his commanding officers saw him come down from the watchtower. They ran to follow him into the house and saluted, but made no remarks. They knew him too well to say anything at this moment. He stood there in silence for a moment, then he turned and looked at them with an angry face.

"Go and prepare our army for the Ortaks' crossing the river. Put up trebuchets, ballistas, and catapults by the riverbank that will break down that ragged bridge they are building! I will hold you personally responsible for every Ortak who manages to cross that river," he yelled at them as he hit the table with his right fist.

"How dare they!" He sat down by the table, and his hands shivered.

His officers saluted again before they left the tent to follow his orders.

Commander Kristjan shivered with anger as he sat on

his chair. He was a tall man in his early fifties. He had long hair that had once been jet-black, as was his beard, but grey was becoming more apparent in recent years. He was wearing a brown, studded leather gambeson, brown leather pants, and big, black leather boots. His plated armour was hanging in his tent, to be used in battle.

He was the commanding officer for the defence of Hergia, at the border by White River, facing Antonia. For twenty years he had been at this post by the riverside, ever since he took over from his father. It was a small outpost located upon a hill one kilometre from the river, overlooking the river and the surrounding area.

He had small patrol groups covering the riverbank, from White Lake to the Utanium Mountains.

There had never been any reason to believe that Hergia would be invaded from the south, until now.

One month ago, he received the news that a large number of Ortaks were heading north from Crystal City. Two weeks later, the Ortaks had arrived at the other bank of the river. He had sent reports to his king of their movements. Then, without delay, he had a stronghold built around his post, covering the whole hill. Once news of the approaching army had reached his king, reinforcements had been sent, and the post was now garrisoned by four thousand extra troops, so he now had almost six thousand men-in-arms watching the borders of White River.

White River was wide and deep. It had never been bridged; there had never been a reason for that. The river created the borders, and kept the two kingdoms separated, keeping the peace between them. In recent years, the river had only needed a few guard posts on each side. It was not until the Ortaks invaded Montania that King Oswald saw the need for strengthening the defences by the river. In fact, there had never been so many troops by the riverside as there were now. Days passed, and his men started to come in from their patrols and posts along the river. They watched as the Ortaks built a massive landing on their side of the river, making platforms, to be used for a floating bridge. It could be any day now, thought the commander.

FOLLOWING his commander's orders and leading the Ortak Army into battle was always a noble task, and for Captain Rolanus, it was a great honour. He had full confidence in his commander and his strategy.

It was early morning, when he marched out of the south gate of the stronghold, and down the road leading to Crystal City with a group of two hundred men. The Hergian guards carefully watching every move on the opposite riverbank could not see what was happening on the other side of the stronghold. After six hours going south, they were well out of the line of sight from Hergia, so they stopped there before turning west, waiting for the next group to arrive. Five hours later, the next group joined them, and, as planned, they now headed off toward Deer Valley. They marched through the woodland until dark, then they camped in a remote pasture. One group after another went out the south gate.

Captain Rolanus and his men headed off to Deer Valley early the next morning.

It was as described, a beautiful grassy valley with a river running through it all the way to White River. There, they gathered one group after another, until there were four thousand of them in that valley.

As soon as the last group arrived, they started their preparation for crossing White River. One hundred men were divided into units of twenty each, and each unit built barges, to ferry the army across White River. The rest of the soldiers made a moat and stronghold in case of an attack, then they waited.

While waiting, the captain sent out twenty scouts across White River, to inform him of the situation from the other side of the river. It was late afternoon on the fourth day, and his men were lined up, ready and waiting for his order. He gave his command, and the Ortaks Army of four thousand troops picked up the barges and headed off for the riverbank of White River.

By that time, one of his scouts had returned, informing him that there was no sign of the Hergian Army on the other side of the river. They had all been called to the stronghold.

The Ortaks Army reached the riverbank by sunset. They placed the barges into the river, each carrying fifty men. The scouts had put five lines across the river, which were to be used to drag the barges across.

It took time to ferry four thousand soldiers and their equipment across, and it wasn't until daybreak that the last one had reached the riverbank of Hergia.

They picked up the barges and hid them in the woodland farther inland. Then they started their march to their next location, led by the scouts. By that evening, they reached a camping place on a grassy pasture that the scouts had found earlier. They raised their camp and rested until morning. As they were making camp, a scout approached the captain.

"We have been seen, Captain."

"Who are they?"

"Some hunters and farmers," the scout replied, waiting for an order.

"That was expected," said the captain in a low voice.

"What do you want us to do? Shall we go after them and kill them?" The scout was obviously hesitant to follow through on his own suggestion, but it was his duty to carry out orders.

"No, there is no need for that. You will probably be seen by someone else. We don't need to get involved with the locals. They will have warned the Hergian Army by now anyway," replied the captain, before he turned his speech to one of his officers.

"Double the watch for the night."

The next morning, they marched, heading east, toward the Hergian stronghold. They saw no indication of being followed, nor that they were about to meet the Hergian Army. In fact, all was quiet. The captain had a strange feeling.

Why haven't they approached us? Certainly, they know we are coming by now, he thought as they made camp that evening.

His scouts informed him of people fleeing the area, and that the entire Hergian Army was at the stronghold. Maybe they will take their stand at the stronghold, after all, he thought as he lay down to get some rest before what would undoubtedly be an eventful day.

The next day they kept east, and by midday, they found themselves in woodland north of the Hergian stronghold, just as ordered by his commander.

Captain Rolanus waited until all his men were in their positions, then he gave the signal.

And in offence formation, the Ortaks Army came out from the woods and marched into the field by the north side of the stronghold.

It was a vast grassland between the woodland and the stronghold. Two small streams ran through it; it was used as a pasture for the Hergian Army and their horses. But now, it had been cleared. They had driven all their livestock inside the stronghold when they heard of the Ortaks approaching.

The captain gave a signal to stop when half of his army had stepped out from the woods. They were well out of range from the siege machines, and the arrows, forcing the Hergian Army to take a stand. Over two thousand men in full armour standing in the pastures was a terrible threat to their enemy, even though they were outnumbered.

This is what the Ortaks did. This was their way of war. This is what they were trained for.

They waited for a short while, then they heard a bell ring. The alarm from the watchtowers at the Hergian Stronghold was being sounded.

As soon as the bell stopped ringing, the captain gave a signal, and as one, his four thousand men started to beat their shields with their swords, making a terrifying racket across the field from the stronghold, and it was heard all the way across the river, where their own commander waited.

COMMANDER KRISTJAN WAS HOLDING a meeting in his house, located at the centre of the stronghold, with six of his commanding officers. The news of the Ortaks crossing the river in the west had created fear among his men, and he had sent word to his king, requesting reinforcement. That had been two days ago.

Then, suddenly, the alarm bell at the North wall rang.

They all went quiet and looked up from the map on the table.

Then a soldier came running inside, his eyes rounded with fear.

"The Ortaks are here!" he shouted.

"What do you mean? Are they here already?" The commander looked at the soldier in shock.

The soldier pointed north, gasping for breath.

"Yes, Commander, they came out from the woods." The soldier squeezed his words out between the gasps, desperately trying to regain control.

"Get a grip, man!" yelled the commander.

He looked at his officers, who were obviously alarmed by the news.

"How are they here so soon? I was not expecting them until tomorrow." The commander turned his words to the soldier.

But the soldier had no answer. He just stood there, scared and confused.

The commander rushed out the door, followed by the soldier and his officers. He headed straight to the nearest watchtower on the north wall, where they were ringing the bell. He climbed the stairs, and as he stepped on the landing, he gave the order to stop sounding the alarm.

He looked across the field. What he saw made his blood run cold. All across the field on the north side of the stronghold, soldiers were standing, ready to attack. A wall of shields from thousands of soldiers, reaching into the woodland, was a more unnerving sight than he had ever encountered before. Suddenly, a loud racket coming from the Ortaks overtook every other sound, as they started beating their shields.

He could see from the looks on the faces of the guards in the tower how frightened they were. He realised that they could not face the Ortaks on a battlefield; it was a guaranteed loss.

He turned and called out to his officers who stood below the tower, waiting for his orders.

"Blow the horn and call every man into the stronghold and close the gates. We must defend ourselves until reinforcement arrives."

They rushed off to follow his orders, and he turned again to watch the Ortaks Army across the field.

Most of his men were outside, either watching the Ortaks from the riverbank or doing their daily training in the field south of the stronghold.

They rushed inside as soon as the order came, leaving their posts and the war machines at the riverbank.

It was almost a stampede when they ran inside the stronghold, locked the gates, and took their positions at the wall.

For a while, complete chaos reigned amongst them, but the commanding officers managed to create order inside the stronghold after a few minutes of initial panic.

Then they waited for the Ortaks to attack.

But the attack never came. Instead, they saw the rest of the enemy army as they emerged from the woodland. They surrounded the stronghold and started digging a moat, creating a rampart, and a wooden fence on top of it.

"They are laying the bridge over the river, Commander," one of the guards from the south wall called out.

The Ortaks were locking them in!

Commander Kristjan stood in the watchtower the whole day, watching his enemy.

"We need to ration the food, Gentlemen. It may be a long wait before the reinforcements from Raven Rock arrive," he said in a low voice.

ON THE OTHER side of the river, he heard the bells from the Hergian stronghold, and then the loud racket his men made when they slammed their swords on their shields. This had been arranged as a sign for him, letting him know that they were in place north of the Hergian stronghold.

This was what Commander Triskar had been waiting for. He saw the Hergian soldiers had left their posts, as they ran to join their army, and he saw the mad rush to get inside their stronghold.

It was time for him to make his move. He gave his men a signal by blowing his horn. His men lifted out the floating bridge on the riverbank and placed it in the river.

They had fashioned it with many parts, and by floating it, they were able to place one piece in front of the other. And in a short time, it reached all the way to the other bank of the river. The commander gave his men a signal. With great speed, his men ran over the floating bridge, placing themselves in front of the south entrance of the Hergian stronghold. Out of reach from arrows and war machines, they lined themselves up.

The commander was in the front line crossing. He waited until all his men had crossed, then he gave the order to surround the stronghold.

His plan had worked. He had predicted that the Hergian Army would not take the risk of a battle in an open field against his army. They would prefer to defend from inside their stronghold, hoping he would attack.

But they had been wrong. Why attack? He would only lose his men. Why not just lock them in? This way, he could wait for the Ortaks Army, or starve them to surrender.

By his order, his men began digging a moat and erecting a wooden fence, locking the Hergian Army inside their own stronghold.

He walked amongst his men, as they were raising the fence and placing the war machines alongside the Hergian stronghold. He met up with Captain Rolanus on the other side, and they saluted each other.

"You did a did job, Captain," he said to his old comrade.

"Thank you, Commander. Your strategy worked well."

"They will not attack us from the stronghold, but I do expect their king to send reinforcements, so we should prepare ourselves for that. We should raise a rampart facing north, to defend ourselves when that time comes," said the commander, while he looked north across the field into the woods.

"Yes, Commander, I will see to it."

"You do that, Captain. I must inform our general of what we have done here," he said. He went to his tent across the river, where he sat down and wrote a letter to his general. Then he gave his workers the order to build a stronger wooden bridge across the river, for his general and the Ortaks Army to use when they arrived.

His men were well organised, and they had built their rampart and the wall surrounding the Hergian stronghold after only three days. And the construction of a substantial bridge across the White River was well on its way.

Commander Triskar was pleased.

Now, all he had to do was wait for further orders from his general.

Then a soldier approached him where he stood on the wall at his stronghold, overlooking the river, and watching his workers at the bridge.

"We have received bad news, Commander." The soldier looked frightened.

"What is it, my good man?" asked the commander, angrily.

"Our forces in Salmon Fjord have been attacked."

"They have what?" he yelled.

"They were all killed, my lord." The soldier just stood there, watching his commander, as his face grew red from anger, and he began clenching and unclenching his fists.

It took Commander Triskar a few minutes to regain control of himself. After a long silence, he turned to the soldier again, who still stood there, now terrified of his commander.

"There were no survivors?" he asked in a low voice, realising the general's son was in command there.

"No, not to my knowledge, Commander. They were all killed by some tribe that has landed in the north. They are called Vikings, my lord."

"Vikings!" he replied, turning to face the river again. He stood there quietly for a while, trying to comprehend what his general would say to that news, then he turned to the soldier again.

"You will come with me. I must write a letter to our general, informing him of this news, and it is you who will deliver it," he said as he walked down the steps, heading for his quarters.

KING OSWALD and Queen Gunnfrid sat on their thrones. Every day, they received more news that was disturbing for the king and court. Their lands were being invaded.

First, he received the news of the Ortaks crossing White River, and as he was about to send reinforcement to Commander Kristjan, there was news from the North coast, informing him of a large fleet invading his lands, a tribe that was called Vikings, coming from the areas in the North.

Their king, Haldor The White, had sent him a message, stating his claim over the lands north of the mountains, from Kings Forest and all the lands in Salmond Fjord, along with the North valleys.

His court was getting impatient, especially his son.

"What are we waiting for? Why are we not attacking the invaders?" his son demanded of the court. Amongst them were noblemen, who had lands in the northern valleys and had now lost everything to the Viking invaders. They supported the prince and encouraged those standing next to him, claiming war upon the Vikings was the only course for them to take.

The king sat quietly while his court convinced itself of the necessity of war.

Then Prince Gunthor stepped in front of the throne.

"My king, let me lead the Hergian Army north and reclaim our lands from those invaders. Your court has offered themselves behind this war, and together, we will prevail against those Vikings," he said as he raised his battle-axe above his head, and the court shouted out a war cry in support.

The queen stood up. "I second that, my son. I have no doubt you will prevail against those who have come here to invade our lands." Again, the court shouted out, raising their weapons.

Then the king suddenly jumped to his feet, and with his powerful voice, he called out over his court.

"Then what?"

They all went quiet and looked at their king, as he stood, red in his face, with clenched fists.

"We have an army of sixteen thousand men strong here at Raven Rock. If we send them against the Vikings, we will lose most of them, if not all." His voice rang out as thunder on his court, commanding all who were present to listen. He went quiet for a while, to let his court absorb what he had said, then he went on with his speech, and his anger had not declined.

"The city of Raven Rock would be defenceless, for Ortaks to enter at will. Let me remind you, there are five thousand Ortaks by White River. They have locked our southern army inside their own stronghold.

"And from the report I just received from my scouts, the Vikings have destroyed the Ortaks' stronghold in Salmon Fjord, leaving no one alive.

"There is only one thing we can do, Gentlemen, and that is to strengthen our defences here at Raven Rock, and defend our castle and the people of this city, hoping that our enemies will kill each other.

"I know that many of you have lost lands, and if we are to regain what has been taken from us, then we must wait. Patience often brings rewards." The king sat down again, and the court prattled amongst themselves for a while, then the king finally lost his patience, and spoke again in a loud voice.

"I have had enough of this nonsense for now! You are all dismissed." He stood up and watched them leave the hall, retreating to his quarters.

He called for the scout who had informed him of the Vikings destroying the Ortaks stronghold.

He was sitting by his desk in his quarters, as the scout entered.

"You will go south to White River, and make sure that the Ortaks hear about the defeat at Salmon Fjord."

"Yes, my lord." The scout bowed and left.

The king stood and began pacing the floor of his room, thinking. He finally stopped by the window. His mind was far away, as he gazed over his city.

Knowing that their men lost to another group of invaders, the Ortaks may take their attention elsewhere, and maybe I can create enough tension between them and the Vikings, so they will destroy each other. At least weaken themselves enough for my army to prevail against them, he thought as he drank his wine, staring out the window.

6 SILVER LAKE

Silver Lake was still, hardly a ripple breaking the surface at that moment, as Grimur stood on the east side of the outer wall of Hungerburg Castle, overlooking the lake and the surrounding area. It looks peaceful enough, he thought as the mountains were reflected in the water below.

The castle guard had not seen any movements of Ortaks patrol groups lately, but that did not mean that they weren't lurking about somewhere nearby.

Grimur, along with five other men from Hungerburg Castle, were waiting until dark to be lowered down the castle wall, onto the ground outside, so they could sneak inside the boat shelter unseen.

Hungerburg Castle had never been garrisoned by more than two hundred people at the most, but Captain Gerhard had brought more than eight hundred men with him when he returned from the terrible defeat at Borg Castle earlier that summer.

Silver Lake was by the borders of Great Cape near the Kings Mountains, and this made it easier for the castle to reach out for food, not having to send men into enemy territory in Antonia.

After the Ortaks had taken the capital of Antonia, Crystal City, the lands had been swarming with Ortaks patrol groups, plundering the villages and towns in the area. Hungerburg Castle was on an island in the lake. And the lake created a moat surrounding the castle. It was safe, for now, for those who took shelter there. It would take a massive army to take the castle, and having such a great defending force inside it, would make it harder still.

There was no ground for any type of siege machines to be placed outside the castle for an attacking army, and only a narrow stone bridge where one could land. Hungerburg Castle was a magnificent fortress, but every castle has its weaknesses, and food supplies while under a siege had proven to be this castle's weakness.

The Ortaks had raised a camp and a stronghold on a grassy hillside overlooking the terrain, and they kept the castle under strict surveillance. They sailed around it on boats, outside of the range of arrows, and rode alongside the lake every day, to make it hard for the castle to provide itself with food.

The Ortaks had decided not to attack the castle for now, because of how fortified the castle really was, and their troops were now occupied elsewhere.

But Captain Gerhard knew perfectly well that it was just a matter of time before they would. Until then, they had to wait, and that could take a long time.

The castle had five fishing boats. The captain had his men build a boathouse for the boats on the coast by the north side of the castle, as far away from the land as he could, where they kept the boats locked inside. This way, the Ortaks weren't able to see whether the boats were at the castle or not. That way, they could sneak out at night and sail the lake without being seen.

They would all starve locked inside the castle if they did not get the food they needed, as the Ortaks had planned. Therefore, Captain Gerhard had taken a considerable risk by sending his men across Silver Lake that summer. In the shelter of the night, they sailed the lake on the fishing boats.

They travelled east and all the way until they reached the roots of Kings Mountains, where they had a good hiding place for the boats. Then they crossed the mountains over to Great Cape on foot and moved into the valleys on the other side of the mountains.

Grimur had been selected to lead these dangerous journeys that summer. He was a guard at the castle, born and raised there, and knew the lake and the surrounding territory better than anyone.

He was in his early forties, medium height, muscular build, and an excellent soldier, just like his father and his grandfather had been before him. He was wearing a brown woollen shirt and pants, black leather boots, and a black leather jacket. He was armed with his long hunting knife and a small axe, which were sheathed in his thick leather belt around his waist.

He was now preparing for his fifth journey, and as usual, he had picked out five men amongst the soldiers to accompany him. He needed their help with the boats, and to carry the supplies down the steep slopes by the lake in Great Cape. They also needed to be ready to fight, in case they were spotted by Ortaks scouts.

By nightfall, they were already up on the wall. The castle guards had tightened the end of the rope to a ring that had been fastened in the inner side of the wall, so if the line slipped in their hands for any reason, the men at the other end would not land on the ground below.

As soon as it was dark, Grimur tightened the rope around his waist and went over the edge of the wall, and the guard lowered him down all the way onto the ground.

I will never get used to this, he thought on his way down in the dark. Then the others were lowered down after him, one by one, until they were all on the ground. A seventh man was lowered as well; he was to close the boathouse, to make sure they were able to get out unnoticed.

Grimur waited for the last drop. It was a leather bag, carrying silver coins and other valuables for him to trade for food in Great Cape.

The others had entered the boathouse by the door facing the castle. The boathouse was two metres from the castle wall and about three from the lake. They locked the door behind them. It was pitch-dark inside, but Grimur and the guards knew their way around and managed to find the boats.

The boats were now picked up and taken out one by one, then carried those few steps down to the lake, where they were lowered into the water. Then they were tightened together with ropes, in a row.

This way, the first boat led the others in the dark, so they would not drift away from each other.

Grimur placed himself in the first boat and slowly moved the boats out from the shore, and the guard carefully locked the door behind them from the inside.

The cold night air created a breeze that found its way

inside their clothing, and that, combined with the tension of sailing in the dark trying not to be seen, made them shiver. Slowly but steadily they made their way onto the lake, then Grimur raised the sail on the first boat, and they soon had a good wind taking them across.

It took them most of the night before they reached the mountains. Grimur lowered the sail, and they used the oars to row the rest of the way. Their eyes had gotten used to the dark, and they were able to see the shores, sailing the boats between the cliffs that reached out into the lake.

Silver Lake reached into a valley that was landlocked by high cliffs, leaving the valley isolated. On his first two trips, Grimur had searched for food in the villages in the bottom of the valley, but he realised that he was putting them in great danger by asking them to help Hungerburg Castle with supplies.

There was only one spot in the valley where he could hide the boats, and the fishermen at the village showed him. A small creek between two high rocks provided a place where he could land the boats without being seen.

Grimur found the hiding place shortly before daybreak, and they placed the boats on the sandy shore, in a small creek behind a large cliff.

And to be safe, they dragged the boats farther up on the beach, under a big overhanging oak, and then they covered the boats with branches that Grimur had used on his earlier trips.

They rested for a while and ate some breakfast before they headed up the slope that led them to the pass across the King Mountains.

Grimur had created some connections amongst the locals

in Great Cape on his previous journeys; they helped him gather the food he needed.

Crossing Kings Mountains through the pass was only for those who knew the area well. Being from the area of Silver Lake gave Grimur some leverage. He was well known amongst the people for his good manners and his honesty.

They made their way up the steep slope from the creek to the place Grimur had used for hiding the cargo to be carried down to the boats on foot.

It was a grassy spot in the hillside with a small cave at the end of it, which he had kept hidden by covering it with rocks. He and his men now removed the rocks, and he entered the cave, returning with six bows and quivers full of arrows. He had kept them there for the crossing.

Then they continued on to the path that led them into the wooded mountain slope. They walked the narrow and slippery path. It had rained in the mountains that night, even though there had not been any while they were sailing the lake. They could see the village in the valley below, as they made their way up to the pass.

After three hours, Grimur suddenly stopped. They were now in the pass, on a small cliff overlooking a strong current river coming down in rapids from a narrow canyon in the mountains at the south. He dropped down on his knees. There were footprints coming onto the path from the woodland and heading towards the river.

"Scouts, three of them," he said in a low voice.

"Why do you think that? This could be anybody," said one of his men, looking around nervously.

"It could be, but I doubt it. Those footprints are new, so keep a good lookout for strangers. They might still be near here. The footprints are leading down to the river, so we should head north. I think there is a short route down into the valleys close by," he said as he turned off the path, heading toward a high ridge not far from them. They followed him, and, as he had suggested, they kept a lookout for the owners of those footprints.

He stopped them again as they were going through the woods, bending down once again.

"What kind of footprint is that?" he asked quietly, pointing down, then he raised himself up, looking for more clues. Broken branches and many more footprints surrounded the area. It seemed that whoever owned those footprints had been here in large numbers.

"Those look like wolf tracks, but much bigger—not a bear, and bears do not come in packs anyway," said one of his men.

"There are also footprints from boots of some kind, many of them," said another soldier in his company, looking down, searching for clues like the others. "It is as if they were headed this way, but then they suddenly disappeared," the man added, pointing in the same direction they were heading. He looked at Grimur in confusion and some fear.

"Whatever this is, we better keep on moving. There are no more tracks to be seen anyway," Grimur said, as he resumed walking through the woods. They saw no more of the footprints, and all was quiet in the woods. No birds were heard, just the breeze in the treetops.

"What is that smell?" one of the men asked suddenly with a scowl. They all noticed it. There was a terrible odour filling the air.

An hour later, they reached the ridge, and Grimur turned right through rough, wooded terrain, until they reached the river again, as it took a turn down and over the cliffs. They climbed down the cliff beside a waterfall, then they followed the river for a while in a narrow canyon.

By noon they had reached the spot where the canyon ended, and they were able to see over the landscape ahead. Below them lay a steep, wooded slope, and beyond the slope, they could see the river, as it snaked itself through a grassy flatland. In the distance, smoke could be seen coming up from a village.

Grimur stopped and gave the others an order to do the same. He had a strange feeling that they were being followed. That peculiar smell had seemed to follow them for a while now, though they were not able to see anything that could have been the source of the stench.

He had not taken this route before, so he had never been to this valley before, not even in his days of hunting. He turned, trying to see if anyone was following, looking for an explanation for the feeling he could not seem to shake.

"What is wrong?" one of his men asked.

"I don't know what exactly is wrong. There is something, or someone, following us. I can feel that, but I can't see anything, just that strange smell that seems never to go away. I feel it coming from behind us," he answered in a low voice, looking behind them once more. There was no one there, just the wind making strange sounds as it shook the trees.

"I can feel it too," said one of his men with a quiver in his voice.

"We should try to get to that village before dark," said Grimur, pointing in the direction of the village. The others nodded, and they headed down the slope, following the river.

Maybe it was the thought of being caught by whatever they were smelling, or their fright of running into Ortaks, but something made them start running, faster and faster, down the wooded slope. Suddenly, they heard a loud noise behind them.

Grimur quickly looked over his shoulder, as he darted to his right, avoiding a tree, and what he saw nearly paralysed him, and he almost lost all strength in his legs.

Beasts as big as cattle, in the form of wolves, were coming over the cliff and through the canyon, steaming straight at them, making terrible growling noises as they opened up their mouths. Astride those creatures were some sort of demon-like creatures, waving swords and spears in the air. He had never in his life seen anything that filled him with such terror.

He and his men ran as fast as they possibly could, down the wooded slope, over bushes and through clearings, rushing through trees and jumping over stones as they ran, not even considering stopping and trying to make a stand against those beasts.

And then, finally, they were running into the grassland below the woods, and they ran even faster now that they were on even ground. Then, he heard a loud, terrible cry. He knew a beast had caught up to one of his men and attacked. Another one of his men screamed out only a minute later, and Grimur, more afraid than he had ever been before, ran all the faster, desperate to outrun the horrible beasts.

He ran into a grassy pasture, trying to keep his speed up, despite how short of breath he now was. One of his men passed him, and he watched in horror as a spear hit the man between the shoulders, throwing him forward, and he landed face down in the grassy ground, dead.

There was a small, peaceful pond ahead, and he realised they were heading straight into marshland. No sooner had the thought crossed his mind, his feet were wet, and he found himself sinking with every footstep.

He had to go straight ahead. It was too late to turn and run past the marshy ground, so with all the speed his legs could offer, he ran into the marshes, and all the way into the pond, now half crawling.

A low, grassy hill blocked the view to the village now, and there was no one to be seen in the pasture, not even any live-stock. From the corner of his eye, he saw another one of his man being attacked by the beasts, then he stumbled and fell face down in the water. He came up, gasping for air, and was met with the sound of a terrible scream. He tried to turn to look back, as his body was sinking into the pond.

The muddy bottom of the pond dragged him down, and the ice-cold water now reached his chest. He saw three beasts, with their riders. They were trying to get to him without sinking. One of the Demons had raised his spear to throw, but then something he could not comprehend happened.

The beast and its rider were hit, not by one arrow, but at least a dozen and the others were assailed with a storm of arrows coming from the left side of him. He turned his head to take a disbelieving look, still sinking into the muddy pond, and saw shiny riders in the pastures charging at the herd of beasts that had been following him and his men.

The knights were in large numbers, and they were riding big, powerful horses, killing the beasts more easily than he imagined possible.

It was over in a matter of seconds, and he tried all he could to free himself from the mud, but nothing worked.

At first, he thought the riders would help him, but when he looked back again, they were all gone. More puzzling than that, so were the beasts and all his men. There was no one to be seen!

He lost all hope. The water had now reached his neck, but he was still able to breathe. Slowly, though, the ice-cold water continued to rise. He used his last breath to scream as loud as he could.

Finally, there was no more air, and the water covered his face. He closed his eyes and let the dark, cold world take over.

GRIMUR REMEMBERED WAKING up at some point and finding himself lying across what appeared to be a large rock, and someone was tapping on his back. He remembered throwing up, mostly water. After that, everything was a blank—he must have lost consciousness again.

When he woke up again, he was in a bed inside a dark room, and he thought he heard someone snoring, but he fell asleep again before he could think too much about it.

Daylight was coming in through a small window as he woke for the third time. He managed to raise his head and take a look around inside the room.

It was small, with one bed and a chair and a small table placed under the window. A woman was sitting on a chair by the opposite wall, and she seemed to be sleeping. She was young and beautiful and was wearing a green dress, and had an apron around her waist. He realised that he was completely naked under a woollen blanket that he had been covered with.

He slowly raised himself up and sat on the edge of the bed, and the woman opened her eyes and looked at him.

It was a bit awkward for him, as he sat there, doing his best to cover his privates, but then she broke the silence with a kind smile.

"So, you finally woke up, then."

"Where are my clothes?"

"Your clothes were soaking wet and covered with mud when they dragged you out of the pond," she replied as she got up from the chair. "But we washed them for you while you were asleep." She smiled even more. "I will fetch them for you now." She headed towards the door, and he just nodded.

I must be in the village, he thought as he heard some prattle and traffic outside the window. There was no more time to speculate because the woman was back in the room, now holding his clothes, and another woman was with her, older than she. By the look of it, he guessed her to be the young woman's mother.

The young woman placed his clothes on the bed beside him, then she took a step back. The two of them stood there side by side, smiling, just looking at him. They were happy to see that he was alive.

He sat there, still awkwardly covering his privates with the blanket, wishing they would stop staring. The two women were obviously not leaving, and being a man, he could not just ask them to.

He pulled himself together and swiftly moved both feet onto the floor, keeping the blanket over his privates as he slipped his pants up his legs, still covering his privates with the blanket. Then he carefully put the pants in place as he stood up with an awkward smile. His manhood was safe for now.

He finished dressing, and the two women waited for him

to finish, keeping their beautiful smiles in place the whole time.

He was about to address them when he heard someone come in behind them.

"I heard you were awake," said a big man with a thick black beard. He was wearing brown leather pants and black high boots, a black gambeson, and black leather gloves. That is no farmer, thought Grimur.

"I am Captain Trinfar of the Great Cape Army and the keeper of law in these parts. Who are you, and why did they find you drowning in the pond? First, they thought you were an Ortaks scout, so they sent for me. But by the look of your clothes, I was convinced you are not." He looked searchingly at him and frowned. "Are you a spy?"

"No, I am Grimur. I am a guard from Hungerburg Castle. I was on my way, along with five other men, to buy some food and supplies for the castle. We are under siege. This is not my first journey into Great Cape, but I have never been in this valley before. Before this, I have done my trading in the valleys south from here. What about my men? Are they all dead?"

They looked at each other questioningly.

"What men?" the captain asked. "You are the only one they found in that pond. If the workers had not been on the other side of the hill, looking for a lost lamb, you would have drowned, since no one would have been close enough to hear you scream." He looked at the women, and they nodded.

Grimur tried to think, struggling to remember what happened, and he sat down on the bed again, just staring at the floor.

"After a good meal, you will have to tell me everything," said the captain, and left him with the women.

They showed him the way to the kitchen, where they had food ready to eat. Others now began to come inside and seat themselves on benches that were on both sides of the long table.

Grimur realised how hungry he was, and he barely looked up while he ate. After the meal, three men approached him and placed themselves in front of him. They were young, hardly more than twenty years old.

"You sure can scream," said one of them, smiling.

"Are you the ones who found and saved me?" Grimur wiped his mouth with his right sleeve.

"We sure did," said the talker, still smiling.

"Thank you, Gentlemen. I hope I can return the favour sometime." Grimur nodded, and all three of them grinned at each other, then left suddenly.

A strange bunch, Grimur thought.

Captain Trinfar entered the hall and stopped in front of him.

"If you are finished with your meal, I would like you to come with me. I need to know more about your visit here." His tone was harsh.

Grimur nodded, smiling at the two women and thanking them for the meal before he followed the captain outside.

It was a surprise for him to see the village. He had thought it would be smaller, but this was more like a town. Outside the door stood two guards, waiting for them to come out, and they walked right behind him, as he followed the captain across the street. They entered a two-storey house that must have been used as a pub or a tavern at one time but was now empty.

Grimur looked around with his eyebrows lifted.

"The owner of this establishment is dead. Killed in a duel over a woman," said the captain as he gestured for Grimur to take a seat at a table in the middle of the hall. "You have met the woman. She kept watching over you during the night. Young and fair she is," he added, smiling.

"Whom did he fight? Where is he?" Grimur found this story interesting.

"I hanged him yesterday. He was a horse thief. He stole twenty horses from a gentleman in the valley north from here. We hang horse thieves around here," said the captain in firmly, as he sat down at the other side of the table, and waved to one of his men to give them some ale to drink.

"That woman didn't show any signs of sorrow." Grimur was surprised.

"Why should she? She hardly knew the man, and never liked the innkeeper either." The captain took a big gulp from his ale. "Now, tell me all there is to know about you and why you are here, and where you have done your business around here." He put the jar on the table.

Grimur told him everything about his trip, and the previous trips he had taken, and whom he had done business with. When he had finished his story, the captain remained quiet for a while, looking at him and frowning. Grimur was getting uncomfortable by the time the captain finally spoke.

"This confirms what I have been hearing for the past few weeks, that someone from Hungerburg Castle was buying food and other supplies here in the valleys." He went quiet for a while. "I do not like soldiers, or other people from Antonia, coming here for that or any other reason. For all we know, they might be Ortaks scouts.

"Knowing that Hungerburg Castle is under siege, I have

my orders from the duke to assist the castle as I can." He paused as he took another sip of his ale. After putting his jar on the table again, he looked at Grimur seriously.

"So this is what we will do. I will see to it that you will have your supplies, and then I'll have my men help you carry them across the pass to your boats. Then two of my men will join you and help you with the boats as you cross the lake to the castle. But from now on, you will fetch your supplies from the cave. I will make sure that every fortnight, supplies for the castle will be waiting for you inside the cave. That way, we can leave each other notes and reports inside the cave, but there will be no more passing into Great Cape without my permission." The captain emptied his beer in a final gulp and stood up.

"The two women will take care of you until we have gathered your supplies. I will advise you not to go anywhere until I return. In fact, there will be two of my men standing guard outside their house until you leave for home," he said as he stepped out the door and onto the street.

Grimur followed him outside. He understood that he was not a free man anymore, but it was some consolation that he would get help carrying all the supplies he needed, and would have company crossing the mountains again. After what had happened, he was grateful for that.

7 OUTLAWS IN KING FOREST

*T*he path lay farther to the South than they had thought at first. They stopped on top of a ridge and watched it for a while. They saw how the path disappeared as it made its turn around the bend.

Sliding down the slope and into a creek below, they started running alongside the path, staying out of sight.

They ran through the woods, fast and quiet. Once in a while, they stopped to listen, then they kept on.

They were identical twins. Scouts and soldiers in Queen Egny's army, their names were August and Sigurstein. Their mission was to locate the main camp of the outlaws in Kings Forest, by orders from Sir Brian.

They had left Troll Fjord four days earlier, and they had been on track for two days now, following the lead and the rumours from the folks in this area. They had come across footprints, which had led them farther into the woods.

More signs led them to believe that they were on the right track. They knew each other well enough to be able to keep quiet, efficiently communicating just by looking at each other. They each knew what the other was thinking. That gave them some leverage and came in handy on a mission like this one.

They were wearing light, leather armour, and were both girded with a short sword and a knife. A bow and quiver lay across each of their shoulders.

They were great marksmen and fighters, trained in hand-to-hand combat from early childhood.

After a few hours of running, they stopped on a low ridge. They had not come across any outlaws, but they knew the valley was only two hours away on the other side of a small mountain.

They could smell a campfire.

The path leading into the valley headed up the slope and in the direction of a narrow pass in the mountain, and crossing it led them into the valley.

From now on, they knew they had to be more careful if they were to keep from being spotted by guards.

Carefully, they made their way closer to the pass, and as they reached the edge of the woodland, they saw that the rocky hillside was the only way to enter the pass.

They stopped and hid behind bushes as they scanned the area ahead.

First, they saw nothing, then they spotted a man standing guard high in the mountain pass. They looked at each other and nodded. Waiting for dark was the only option they had.

They sat down to wait. They took turns guarding while the other one napped. They would need their strength if they were to cross the path during the night.

At sunset, they stretched themselves and ate some dried

meat. As soon as it was safe, they headed up the hillside, climbing the rocky slope without making a sound.

As they approached the area where they had spotted the guard, they saw a small fire, and two men sitting by it, leaning against a large rock.

They had almost gone too far but were able to come to a standstill in time to avoid detection, when one of the guards suddenly stood up to relieve himself of his urine.

He walked a few steps in their direction and started urinating, mumbling something to himself.

He was too busy to notice the two men standing not more than twenty metres away from him.

He looked up when an arrow split the air, hitting him straight in the heart.

He made no sound before he fell facedown.

However, the sound of his body hitting the ground was loud enough for the other guard to jump to his feet by the fire. But by that time, another arrow made its way from the surrounding darkness, and he fell dead before he could see who killed him.

The brothers took the bodies and placed them by the fire, leaning them up against the big rock, sitting as they were before.

After that, they kept on with their journey. It was pitch-dark, but following the muddy floor of the path made it easier to find their way. They had made their way across within a few hours. As they stood up on the top of the pass, overlooking the valley below, they were able to see the glow from the campfires that were scattered across the valley floor beneath them.

They decided to wait for daybreak, to have a better view

over the valley and the terrain. They concealed themselves behind a rock and waited.

By daybreak, they were able to see the landscape clearly. There was no one to be seen outside yet, only the livestock in the pastures.

The valley lay from east to west, and it was surrounded by mountains on all but the east side, where a river with a strong current blocked the path into the valley.

Lukas had chosen an excellent spot for his main camp. It was almost impossible to attack him with an army. An army would have to cross the river, and would probably endure significant casualties.

Closing the pass, they crossed earlier was easy on the other side. The steep slope up to the pass would make a defence simpler if an army approached from that side.

Either Lukas was a good commander, or he was just lucky when he chose the valley for his home. They estimated that there were at least four hundred men, women, and children in the valley.

The only fences they saw were used to keep the livestock inside, but no military structures of any kind were in sight. Lukas was not expecting any siege.

There were all sorts of dwellings in the valley, from big, well-built houses, down to tents, but mostly, there were huts. As they sat there watching the valley below, people were beginning their day, coming out of the cabins and tents, making fires and tending to the livestock.

They had seen enough and were about to turn back to give their report, wanting to make sure they would not be spotted. It was then they saw five riders, travelling fast out of the camp. The riders crossed a small stream and moved onto the path that led up the slope and into the pass.

They had no other choice than to stay behind the rock and let the riders pass. They flattened themselves on the ground behind a small bush, not more than twenty metres from the path, and waited until the riders had passed. Then they carefully made their way, until they were out of sight from the outlaws' camp, then they hurried after the riders, making sure that they were not seen.

As they ran back across the pass, it began to rain, making it harder to keep up with the riders. They realised that when the riders saw the guards were dead, at least one of them would sound an alarm.

They had been right, and after a while, they saw two riders approaching. The riders increased the speed of their horses and drew their swords.

Without any hesitation, the twins drew their bows and aimed at the men, not backing down.

The riders had about twenty metres till impact when the two arrows were shot simultaneously. One fell backwards off his horse, dead, but the other one managed to stay in his saddle, despite the arrow embedded in his body. The twins lifted their hands to stop the horses, and the rider who still sat in his saddle fell off the horse. He was stone dead.

The twins estimated that they were only half an hour's ride from where they killed the guards, and the other riders were probably waiting there for backup from the valley.

They mounted the horses and headed through the pass as fast as the animals could carry them. They each leaned forward in their saddle, so the heavy rain and the gusty wind would not be as hard on them as it drafted through the mountain pass.

When they had the post in sight, they saw where the

other three men had dismounted their horses and were making graves for the dead guards.

The brothers drew their swords. It came as quite a surprise to the three men when they attacked them. The outlaws had no skills that had any hope of matching the brothers in combat, and two of them fell dead within moments. The third one started running up the mountain slope, trying to get out of their reach, but an arrow released from August's bow put a swift end to that.

The twins changed horses so they would have fresh mounts as they continued their journey, then they headed off again, without any more delay.

They calculated that it would take them two days to reach the farm where they had left their own horses and another day before they reached Sir Brian at his camp at Troll Fjord.

They followed the path through the woodlands and tried to go as fast as the horses could carry them, without over-tiring them.

After four hours, they stopped in a clearing by the road to let the horses rest for a while. They thought themselves safe now, as they sat down on the grassy ground. August smiled at his brother. They had been lucky and were glad to be on their way home again. Sigurstein nodded in content-ment and smiled as he bent down to pick up the horse's reins that had slipped out of his hand.

Suddenly, he heard a smooth sound just above his head, and before he looked up, he knew what it meant.

He turned his head and saw an arrow sticking out of his brother's chest. Frozen, his mouth half open, he sensed someone coming at him from his left side.

Unconsciously, he drew his sword to protect himself.

With a swift move, he blocked a blow coming at him, as the attacker tried to hit him with an axe.

He saw three other men about ten metres away. One of them was placing an arrow in his bow. In a few steps, he approached the archer at high speed, and in one blow, he cut his head off. Seeing his brother shot, he lost all control of his emotions.

Blinded with grief and wrath, he attacked the other outlaws, and before they could comprehend what happened, he had cut them all down.

He ran to his brother, desperate to see that he was okay. The arrow had penetrated his heart, and there was no sign of life—there was no hope. He knelt down beside him and gathered his brother's body in his arms as he wept bitterly. It wasn't until an hour had passed that he managed to pull himself together. Steeling himself, he tied his brother's body across the horse August had been riding, then he mounted his own horse and headed off again. He needed to give his report to Sir Brian.

FROM THE REPORT given to him by Sigurstein, and after he interrogated him for an hour, Sir Brian made his final decision. He would attack the outlaws by crossing the river.

The next day, he led his army in the direction where Lukas and his outlaws had made their camp. He was going to get rid of those outlaws once and for all.

He had two hundred fifty men-in-arms, well-trained and ready for battle, while Lukas had just a ragged crowd, men of all ages and women. They would be no match for his men.

Sigurstein led the way. He had buried his brother three days earlier. Their friends and their army comrades had given him an honourable burial, and all had paid their respects to him. Still, grief weighed heavily on him, a burden almost too heavy to bear, and he was eager for revenge.

The path to the outlaws' valley lay through rough terrain in Kings Forest. Rocky hills, strong current rivers, and swamps were some of the things they had to cross on their way. Finally, after a four-day march, they reached the outskirts of the forest, and across the pasture in front of them lay the river at the end of the valley. Sigurstein had led them directly to the right spot in the woods by the pasture.

Sir Brian signalled his men to stop. For a while, he just looked across the pasture, across the river, and up the valley.

He did not say much, but it was evident when he looked at Sigurstein, that he was determined to avenge his brother, along with so many others Lukas had killed.

The river blocked the entrance into the valley, just like Sigurstein had told him in his report. The day before, Sir Brian had sent thirty men to the pass where the twins had killed the two guards. They were to make sure the outlaws couldn't escape that way. All was quiet. Maybe it was too quiet. They were well hidden in a wooded area, only one hundred metres from the river. He had a good view up into the valley from where he was standing, but it looked like it had been deserted. There was no one to be seen outside the huts, or in the pastures.

Where are all the people? He gave a signal, and five of his men crossed the clearing. They managed to reach the river, without any interruptions. Still, there was no sign of the outlaws.

As soon as he had headed off from Troll Fjord four days

earlier toward the valley, he had sent scouts ahead, but they had reported that there was no sign of outlaws on their way. So it came as a surprise to him, to see that the valley was empty.

Only huts and tents, and some livestock in the pastures remained. There was no sign of people about.

Where were the outlaws?

He waited for a while, not sure what to do. He worried this might be a trap, but he would never know without trying.

So he gave his men a signal, and they all stepped out from the woods into the field, holding their shields in front of them as a protection against a possible ambush. They stopped on the riverbank. Still no sign of the outlaws. Something is wrong, he thought.

The river was about seventeen metres wide, but deep, and had a strong current, making it hard to cross.

Ten of his strongest swimmers tied ropes around their waists and swam across the river, creating safe-lines for the others to use in their crossing.

After they secured the safe-lines, he and his men started crossing the river. He waded into the cold water, a bit surprised by the strength of the current, but he had a good grip on the safe-line, so slowly, he went deeper and deeper. Everything was going well, but when he had only ten metres before he would reach the other bank, he suddenly heard his men screaming behind him. By that time, the water was about waist-deep, and he was struggling to stay on his feet, holding the safe-line as the current continually pushed at him.

He turned to see what had happened. Finally, it was clear why the valley was deserted.

Behind them, coming out of the woodland, was a large number of outlaws, and not as ragged as he had imagined.

Then he realised they had walked into a trap. The outlaws had evacuated the valley as soon as they had realised that their hiding place had been discovered by the twins. They must have been staying out of sight, just waiting for them to cross the river. These were their woods; no one could sneak around them without them knowing, especially a group two hundred strong.

And now Sir Brian and his men had made themselves almost defenceless against their attack, their strength was taken by their struggle against the current.

The outlaws' army had released their arrows, and Sir Brian barely managed to raise his shield, before a hail of arrows landed on him and his troops in the river.

He slipped and fell into the water, as one of the arrows hit him in the left shoulder. Gasping for air, he saw his men dying all around him, some trying to keep themselves floating as the current grabbed them, carrying them downstream.

He lost his grip on the safe-line and sank, as the current dragged him downward.

He managed to grab another safe-line and was trying to stand up when another arrow hit him. This time in the right thigh.

He screamed in pain and grabbed his thigh as the third arrow hit him in the chest. It went through his armour, and he saw the archer on the riverbank holding a big longbow. Somehow, he knew it was Lukas.

That was the last thing he saw, as he fell into the river, dead.

Like Sir Brian had thought, as soon as Lukas heard of

the twins scouting near his valley, he gave the order to the outlaws to abandon their homes and head out to a hiding place a half day's ride from the river. After that, he waited for the royal army to approach the river.

All went just as planned. When more than half of the soldiers were either in the river or across it, he gave his men the signal they had been waiting for.

They lifted their bows and sent a storm of arrows at their enemy, first aiming at the men on this side of the river, then on the men crossing. It came as a complete surprise to them, and there was no time for them to make a defence before the arrows began to cut them down.

Lukas had four hundred men organised for his attack, and they managed to kill most of the soldiers with their arrows. He ran to the riverbank, to see Sir Brian in the river, and shot him down personally.

The battle was over when he looked at his men. Only a few of the soldiers, who had managed to cross the river, had escaped death. He gave an order, and a large number of outlaws surged into the river, to hunt down the men who had escaped. They were not to let the soldiers get away and give a report of what had happened here.

One of the soldiers was Sigurstein. He had been one who swam across with the safe-lines. He saw his fellow soldiers being butchered by the outlaws, and he knew they would come after those who had managed to cross the river and were still alive. He also knew the importance of a report being made about the ambush. For that to happen, at least one of them must survive.

He ran up the valley along with thirty of his fellow soldiers. Many of them still had their armour on, so running for a long distance was quite hard for them.

However, for those who swam across with the safe-lines, it was easier. They had removed their armour, and were only in light clothing, and had tied their weapons on their backs.

Sigurstein still had his weapons. His knife, sword, and his bow and quiver, and running was one thing he was good at.

He aimed at the pass he had crossed earlier, hoping to outrun the outlaws following. Once in a while, he heard his fellow soldiers scream, hit by an arrow, and he realised that they were all getting too tired to keep up with him.

He was hoping the men Sir Brian had sent to the pass the day before were just up ahead. He ran through the pastures, and then uphill, followed by the soldiers who were still alive, and on their heels were the outlaws.

It was every man for himself. The outlaws were too many to stand against in combat, so the only chance they had was to outrun them.

Finally, he reached the spot where he and his brother had been spying on the outlaws during their scouting mission, then he came to the path that went through the pass.

He ran even faster now, and he knew, without looking back, that he was gaining ground. If only he could reach the woodland on the other side of the pass, then he would have a great chance of escaping.

As he approached the other end of the pass, he saw the soldiers Sir Brian had sent the day before. They were all dead, and most of them had been hung up in the trees, probably as a sort of warning.

He passed them without slowing down. He ran through the hill-slope, but instead of following the path, he ran off to the left and into the woodland on the mountain slope.

It was a dangerous move. He did not know the land or

the mountainside well enough, but, on the other hand, following the path, he would inevitably run into the outlaws.

After running the woodland for half an hour, he suddenly found himself on a ledge overlooking the landscape. Down below, he could see the woods, and he thought he saw movement between the trees.

He had no idea whether anyone had seen him, but he took no chance. He turned and ran higher up the mountain, then found some trees to hide within.

He sat there the rest of the day, watching the lands below and catching his breath.

He realised he had outrun them. No one came after him. They had probably followed his comrades down the path, or so he hoped.

Several hours later, after the sun had set, all was dark. After giving it some thought, he decided to take the chance and climb down the cliff, using the darkness to his advantage. It was a bold move but was the only chance of getting down from the mountain, without being seen that he could think of.

He inched down the cliff, moving slowly but steadily, and after about an hour, he found himself down on the forest floor.

He stood still for a moment, waiting and listening to the sounds of the forest, in case he had been seen or heard, but there was no sign that he was not alone.

Then he started walking through the woods, slowly and carefully, stopping every now and then, to be sure that he was not being followed, or walking into another ambush.

By morning he found himself in a clearing. He recognised the area from his previous trip, and that gave him some confidence. He was sure that he was not being followed. He rested by a small pond, and when he looked at his hands, he saw that they were shaking.

He was angry at himself, for leading Sir Brian and his army into an ambush. I should have known better, he thought. It was late, and he was tired, so he decided to rest for the night by the pond. Early the next morning he headed off to Troll Fjord.

He was able to hunt for food with his bow, and that helped him to make his way through Kings Wood, and four days later, he had reached the village in Troll Fjord.

8 THE SIEGE AT CASTOR CASTLE

*C*ommander Triskar rode his horse across the bridge they had built over White River. It had been seven weeks since his army had surrounded the Hergian stronghold.

His workers had just finished building the bridge across White River, which had replaced the floating bridge they used to invade Hergia. He was returning from his daily patrol with his guard, now heading his way to Antonia's side of the river, when one of his soldiers approached him on the bridge.

"A messenger has arrived from Crystal City, Commander. He is waiting by your tent." The commander did not reply but immediately turned his mount towards his tent, followed by his soldier.

As he approached his tent, he saw a man standing in front of it with a horse, holding the reins, obviously waiting.

The commander stopped his horse and dismounted. He

handed his reins to one of his guards, then turned to the newcomer.

"You have a message for me?"

"Yes, Commander." The messenger removed a bag that he had across his shoulders, then handed it to the commander.

"From General Akhtar," he said and bowed a little.

The commander reached into the bag and found a letter.

"You may find a place to rest and eat now, but do not leave the camp. I need you to return to Crystal City with a reply," said the commander before he stepped inside his tent.

He sat down at his table and started reading the letter from his general. It was an order, simple and firm. He was to attack and defeat Castor Castle and make the castle the headquarters for the Ortaks Army in Hergia.

He put the letter on the table, thinking. There was no mention of reinforcements. He had five thousand men, surrounding seven thousand in the Hergian stronghold, and he was expected to defeat the castle that was at least three days' march from his camp as well.

"Get me the scout from the West lands, the one who was here last week," he told his guard, who stood inside the tent, waiting for his orders. Then he stood up to find the map of the terrain. He laid the map on the table and stared at it for a while, his mind elsewhere.

What does the general have in mind? He knows how many men I have. We have been here laying siege around the Hergian stronghold all this time, and now he wants me to leave with part of our army and march for three days to attack a castle? He must have something in mind. His thoughts were interrupted as the scout entered the tent. The commander looked up from the map and turned to face him.

"What can you tell me about Castor Castle?"

"What I have already told you, Commander. It is a fortress that is built upon a high ridge, and the only way to enter the castle is from the North side, through the main gate," the scout said, obviously surprised by the question.

The commander nodded, looking at the map. "So you have told me, but is there no other way?" He looked up from the map, staring at his scout intently. "How is the West side protected?" he asked.

"Well, on the West side of the castle, there is a high mountain, and the area between the mountain and the castle is covered with large rocks. There is no way to use that terrain for an attack. The castle walls are very high, and a deep ditch lies underneath, so siege towers or other war machines cannot be used, Commander." The scout was still confused by these questions.

"What about trebuchets, catapults, or ballistas, can we use any of those on the West side?" The commander was beginning to get a bit angry. Was his general not informed of the defences of this particular castle, the castle he was demanding they conquer? It seemed, at this point, as if he was being sent on a mission of failure.

"If war machines were to be used in an attack on the West side, they would have to be assembled on the ground, where they are to be used. There is no way to wheel them into that terrain. And even so, it is a rough terrain for a foot soldier to cross. There will be no running at the wall. Then there is the climbing up onto the castle wall. The men would first have to go down into a deep ditch before they would be able to raise their ladders. And the floor of that ditch is so rocky that raising the ladder would be almost impossible, Commander." The scout stopped talking, still wondering why his commander would want to know such details. Surely he was not considering an attack on Castor Castle?

Commander Triskar could not take his eyes from the map. His thoughts were even angrier than before.

"I have heard enough. You will leave now, and you will get me more information about that castle and the surrounding terrain. You are dismissed." The commander frowned as he sat down by the table again.

This is a tight situation you have put me in now, my general. What do you really want? He shook off his thoughts.

"Guard! Call my council for a meeting, and fetch me some food. I'm starving!" he called out, as he removed his plate armour.

JOHN, Duke of Castor, was having his breakfast when one of his guards stepped inside his quarters and greeted his master.

"What brings you into my quarters at this time of a day?" said the duke, discontent apparent in his tone.

"Bad news, my lord," replied the man, waiting for permission to say more.

"Oh, what news is that?" The Duke reached out to take a slice of bread from the table.

"A scout has arrived, bringing us the news of an army of Ortaks heading this way, from their stronghold at White River," replied the guard.

The duke paused at his breakfast. "Bring the scout into the hall. I want to question him myself." He leaned back in his chair at the breakfast table. "And ask Captain Harleff to join us at the meeting," the Duke added, already in deep thought, looking at the food on the table.

"Yes, my lord will do." The guard bowed and left the room.

This is sooner than expected, thought the duke while finishing his breakfast. He stood up from the table and headed into his sleeping quarters. His servant placed his cape on his master's shoulders and tied the laces on his black leather shoes. Then the servant stepped back as a sign that he had completed his task, and his master was ready.

The duke stood there without saying a word. He was an elderly man, and his grey, well-combed beard reached his chest. He was not a man who could lead his men into battle any more, but he had good men and knights, who would carry out the task for him. He knew that.

His king had made it perfectly clear that he would not divide his army and send reinforcement if any of his castles or military structures were under attack. He would keep his army at Raven Rock to defend the capital.

But then, his lordship also knew now that the Ortaks were not invincible as many had thought; they could be beaten just like everyone else.

The whispering and the prattle amongst his closest advisers immediately silenced when he entered the main hall. He took his place in his chair overlooking the hall. A man in his early forties stood in the middle, and as the duke sat down, he approached him and bowed.

"You summoned me, Your Lordship," the man said, casting his eyes onto the floor.

"Are you the scout who is bringing us the news of Ortaks heading this way, and if so, what can you tell us, exactly?" The duke looked at the man with searching eyes.

"Yes, Your Lordship, I am a scout in the royal army, and I was the one who brought you the news. The Ortaks are heading this way with three thousand men strong, mostly foot soldiers. They left their stronghold by White River two days ago, and should be arriving here within two more days, Your Lordship." The man spoke loud enough for everyone to hear.

The duke sat there, quiet, for a while, trying to comprehend the news he had been given. Three thousand men is a strong army, especially when we are only four hundred, counting every worker and elderly, anyone, in fact, who could shoot a bow. But we must defend, he thought.

"Is there anything else that you can tell me about this army?" the duke asked, and those in the hall were able to hear a slight tremble in his voice.

"Only that this is a well-organised and well-trained army. They seem to be carrying war machines with them, or so we think," the scout answered.

"What do you know about their commanding officer?"

"From what we know, they are led by Commander Triskar, one of the most experienced officers in the Ortaks Army, my lord."

The Duke frowned. That was not good news at all. He thought for a while, then turned his speech to his court.

"What do you suggest, Gentlemen? Do we flee, or do we make a stand and defend?"

This was not a question, they all knew that. The duke was just testing out the fighting spirit amongst his men.

His court raised their weapons as one and shouted.

"We will fight!"

The Duke nodded his head in satisfaction, then he turned his words to the scout again.

"You go now to your king, and give him my best, and you tell him that Duke John of Castor and his loyal servants will defend at his castle." The scout bowed and left the hall. The duke turned his words to Captain Harleff.

"You will open up our gates for those fleeing the Ortaks, but you will also prepare our defences. We can expect a long siege, Gentlemen." Those last words, he directed to his court.

Castor Castle was massive, towering over the terrain, from up on a high hill. On both the East and the South side, the hill ended in a big, vertical rock. The outer wall of the castle was built out on the edge of it, where the castle wall became an extension of the cliff. At each corner of the wall, was a bastion standing out from it, to create a stronger defence for the castle.

From the day the duke heard about the Ortaks raising a stronghold on the other side of White River, he realised that it was only a matter of time before they invaded Hergia. Therefore, he had his men build an overhang, more than two metres wide, on the edge of the outer wall.

So even if the enemies were able to climb up, first the rock, then the wall, they would be trapped at the overhang. But even that was unlikely to happen.

Water was dripping out of the cliff in many places, making it slippery, and almost impossible to climb. And anyone trying would be an easy target for archers at the bastions.

At the West side of the castle, there was a rough terrain, one kilometre wide, between Castor Mountain that rose one thousand metres high above the castle hill.

That terrain was mostly covered by large rocks that had fallen from the mountain through the ages. In addition to that, a wide, deep ditch had been dug at the time the castle was built, so there was no way for an attack force to use siege machines of any kind from that side of the castle.

The only way for the Ortaks to attack the castle would be from the North, at the front gate, but even there, they would face a significant obstacle. There was a narrow road that led up to the castle and ended in a steep ramp and a drawbridge, that lay across a deep, broad ditch instead of a moat in front of the Barbican.

That was the outer wall. The keep was back at the edge of the cliff on the southern side, and another drawbridge lay across another ditch by the curtain wall, so if by any chance, an army was able to get inside over the outer wall, the keep itself was a strong fortress and would have to be conquered.

That is why the North side was the only effective way for the Ortaks to attack Castor Castle.

Captain Harleff did as his master asked. He kept the gate open for those who sought shelter from the Ortaks, and for the next two days, people from nearby villages and valleys fled to the castle, fearing for their lives.

Then, by nightfall, they saw the Ortaks as they approached from the East in long rows, all three thousand of them, carrying torches in the dark.

It was a terrifying sight, and they continued to stare as the Ortaks entered the valley below the castle, into the villages, then the fields and pastures.

In the still of the evening, they heard the Ortaks, as they were making camp, then they saw the campfires when they lit them one by one. Only one hour later, the whole valley was covered with burning lights from the enemy campfires.

Duke John gave his order, and they lifted the castle drawbridge and closed the barbican door. The duke stood upon the castle wall, watching the campfires below, and he wrapped his cape tighter across his neck in an attempt to stave off a chill that had nothing to do with the temperature. The autumn breeze blew cold air under his clothing, and he was in deep thought.

So many things had changed since he first heard of the Ortaks from Sir Klaus and Commander Christian, his saviours, but they had left his castle a little over a year ago. Arnar, the young boy from the small village by White Lake, had stayed with him.

Arnar had proved himself to be a hard-working young man, and the duke had kept his eye on him during the time he had been here.

At first, the young man had been in the service of one of his knights, but the knight had died on a hunting trip a few weeks ago, so the duke decided to take the young man into his own service. He would make him a squire as he grew old enough to handle himself against trained fighters.

The war machines had been lined up in the bailey by the North wall, six trebuchets and eight catapults, each capable of throwing heavy rocks as missiles over the wall. And twelve ballistas, each armed with forty arrows. All were armed and waiting to be launched.

He had, at this moment, four hundred men and women well armed and most of them well trained, and about one hundred men, women, and youngsters, to be used as archers upon the wall, mostly on the South and the East side.

There was tension in the air, as those who were not standing watch that night tried to get some sleep. The refugees had lit campfires inside the bailey, where they warmed themselves.

The duke had a hard time falling asleep that evening. He was afraid, not just for his own life, but for all his men and women. What will the Ortaks do with the children if they prevail? Will they kill them too? He just lay there thinking, and the more he thought, the more frightened he became.

The next morning a guard entered His Lordship's quarters and informed him that there was a man on a horse down the road.

"What do you mean?" the duke asked, lifting his eyebrows.

"My lord, he is just sitting there," the guard replied as he cast his eyes at the floor, frightened at his master's reaction to the news.

The duke continued staring at the guard with empty eyes, thinking, before he finally spoke.

"I must see that for myself."

He followed the guard outside and up the stairs to the North wall. Captain Harleff stood there above the gate, and as the Duke approached him, he bowed for his master. Then the duke looked over the wall and down to the road leading up to the castle. He saw the man clearly, as he sat there in his saddle.

"How long has he been there?" asked the Duke, not taking his eyes off the rider.

"At least half an hour, my lord," replied the captain.

"What do you think he's doing, Captain?"

"I think he is evaluating his position and our defences, my lord."

"Has he approached, or set any demands?" asked the duke in a low voice.

"No, my lord. He is just laying out his plans on how to best attack us."

"How do you know that, if he has not spoken to you, Captain?" A bit of sarcasm was in the duke's voice.

"Because, my lord, that is what a commander would do." The captain kept his tone calm, intent on acting as if he did not hear his master's sarcastic tone.

"And what would you do, if you were about to attack this castle, Captain?" asked the duke, the sarcasm now gone.

"That is hard to say, my lord, but the front gate is the only way to enter, so that is what he will probably focus on. I am sure he will also try to distract us in some way while doing so." The captain turned his eye to the rider.

They stood there silently for a while, watching the rider, who still sat there, in the middle of the road. Suddenly he went off the road and headed to the West side. He stopped his horse there for a while, then he turned up on the road again, and took a look at the castle before he went back down the road into the valley.

His Lordship watched the rider disappear behind the trees, then he turned to Captain Harleff.

"We do not know when the Ortaks will attack, Captain, but I am giving you full command of the defence of this castle. I will return to the keep and maintain a good spirit over the women and the children when the fighting begins."

COMMANDER TRISKAR HAD HOPED they would reach the castle before dark, but they still had an hour's walk to the fields and the pastures of Castor Valley, when the darkness came. They lit their torches and kept on with their march.

It had been three days since they left their camp by White River, headed out for Castor Castle. He left the camp leading three thousand men, leaving two thousand soldiers at the siege by White River.

He knew he was stretching his army to the brink of breaking, but he also knew that the fighting spirit of the Hergian Army while surrounded in their own stronghold was as low as it could get.

He was the only one on horseback on this march. He wanted to keep the rest of the cavalry at the stronghold. Horses had no purpose in a siege of a castle.

He left his most trustworthy man, Commander Rolanus, in charge of the siege by White River in his absence. He knew he could count on him to stand against the Hergians, if they tried an outbreak from their stronghold.

At first, the commander and his men marched west, alongside White River, then, on the second day, they turned north, onto the road that led them to Castor Castle.

As they reached the valley below the castle in the dark, he gave his men the order to set up camp.

As he looked up, he could see small lights coming through the loops of the castle that reigned with all its might, quietly dignified upon the high hill. I will have to wait until morning to see what we are up against, he thought as he dismounted his horse.

His men raised his tent, and one hour later, he had a council meeting with his commanding officers. After detailing the fundamental grounds of the siege from the information they had, he dismissed the meeting and lay down on his bed to rest.

By first light, he had been awake for some time and stepped outside. Standing in front of his tent, he looked up the hill and all the way to the castle towers. His scouts had been right, there was no way of attacking the castle from this side of the valley. He looked north. The valley lay farther north than he could see from where he stood, and from what he had been told, the road that led to the castle gate lay at the Northside.

He asked for his horse, and after mounting, he made his way north, through the campsite that his men had made the night before, and all the way to the road that led the way to the castle. He travelled through three villages in the valley. His men were already there. The villages were all empty. The people had fled, seeking refuge in the castle. His men had raided the villages and taken all they needed, but when he asked one of the guards, he told them that there had been no food, only clothing, hand tools, and some weapons. There were some farmhouses and livestock in the pastures; other than that, the valley was empty.

"They must have taken what food they had with them when they fled into the castle," said the guard.

After a short meeting with his commanding officers, giving them their orders for the day, he mounted his horse again and took the road up to the castle.

When he approached the main gate, he was able to have a better overview of the castle's entrance. He stopped far enough back to be out of range from the archers and war machines, but close enough to see where the road ended by the ramp and how narrow the ground was for his men to attack.

He sat there astride his horse for some time, thinking. The only way for him to get his men over the walls of this castle was at the gate in the siege towers, and from the look of it, they would only be able to get one tower to the wall at a time. It would have to be a big tower, and the landing bridge would have to be a long one, for it had to be played over the ditch, and onto the wall above the Barbican.

He lost track of time sitting there thinking, but finally, he turned his horse west and left the road. He wanted to examine the area on the West side of the castle, but as his scout had already explained to him, it was rough terrain, and there was no chance they would be able to get siege machines in place there. Still, we will need to attack the West wall, if only to give our attackers a chance at the front gate, he thought.

He went back to the road and sat there in his saddle for an hour more, thinking. His horse was getting restless, and still, he sat. Eventually, he turned his horse and headed down the road and into the camp.

His commanding officers had been waiting for him by the road to the castle, having already carried out the orders he had given them earlier. He stopped his horse in front of them on his way back. He did not dismount but gave them his orders from astride the beast.

"Raise a siege tower, and assemble four catapults from the pile of war machines we brought with us. We will attack the castle at daybreak tomorrow," he said, then he turned to look at the castle one more time before he rode down into the valley and to his tent.

He stopped in front of his tent and turned his words to one of his guards.

"Fetch me a messenger. I need to send our general a report," he commanded as he gained the privacy of his tent.

An hour later, he had written his report to his general, and the messenger was on his way to Crystal City. He stepped outside his tent again, and once more, he took a good look at the castle. If the Ortaks were to make Hergia theirs, they would have to defeat that castle.

~

A THICK MIST lay over the valley the next morning when the Ortaks lined themselves up beside and behind the siege tower. They had taken their places inside the tower, ready to push it uphill on the road leading to Castor Castle. They waited for the signal to be given for the attack.

Upon the castle walls, the guard waited as well. They had watched the day before, as the Ortaks raised the siege tower down in the valley. And they had seen when they placed it on the road leading to the castle. The castle guard knew that it was just a matter of time before the tower would start to move towards the castle.

The fear of what was coming grew stronger every minute, as the people who had fled their homes in the valley waited for the Ortaks to attack.

All was quiet that morning, as the castle guard stared into the mist, though there was nothing to be seen or heard for a long while. Then, the sound of a horn coming down from the valley echoed through the mist. Loud and scary, the sound pierced the morning air. The men at the castle wall shivered with fear.

The mist was not only thick, but it was cold. Then the castle guards heard the sound of the wheels, as the siege tower was slowly pushed up the road, coming closer and closer.

The people down in the bailey ran inside the keep, frightened for their lives, and the door was closed behind them, as they took shelter.

Captain Harleff had been given the full command in defence of the castle by the duke, and he stood upon the wall by the Barbican. Like the rest of them, he strained to see the tower or the enemy as they approached. At first, he saw nothing. But after a while he managed to see the outlines of the tower, as it appeared in the mist, slowly making its way up the road. His nerves were expanded to their limits, and he could feel his legs shaking as he waited. Then, finally, the tower reached the spot on the road that he and his men had measured for the trebuchets. And he lifted his hand, as a signal to his men at one of the trebuchets.

They launched their missile, a large rock. He followed the rock with his eyes as it took off, flying through the air towards what he hoped would be a painful blow to the enemy. First, it was as if the rock was going straight up, but it took a gentle curve, and as he had hoped, it landed on the siege tower. It made a hole in the tower almost at the top, and Captain Harleff raised his hand again, and the rest of the trebuchets, all five of them, launched their rocks as well.

Two of the rocks missed the siege tower completely, but they landed within the ranks of Ortaks who were pushing the tower. The other three stones hit their mark, smashing most of the tower to pieces.

Only the lower part with the wheels remained. The Ortaks stopped at the sound of a whistle, and after another whistle sounded, they began to move what was left of the tower back down the road. Only a few minutes later, however, the guards on the castle wall saw they had pulled catapults and ballistas up the road towards the castle. They had not finished their attack on the castle, though the destruction of the tower had been swift and brutal.

The commander by the trebuchets had reloaded the trebuchets by this time, and after a signal from Captain Harleff, they launched the rocks upon the enemy once again. The guard on the wall watched as the rocks landed. Two of them hit their marks, smashing a catapult and a ballista into pieces, but three rocks fell upon empty space, though one may have landed on some of the Ortaks soldiers. The Ortaks drew closer, slowly, but at a firm and steady pace, advancing towards the castle wall. They lined the war machines up on the road and the area around it, so they were able to aim them at the castle wall. A large group of soldiers went out of reach, moving around to the West side into the rough terrain, carrying long ladders with them.

Captain Harleff gave his men at the catapults a signal, and they launched the stones, shooting them over the castle wall, eager to do as much damage to the enemy's war machine, and their soldiers, as possible.

As soon as the catapults at the castle had shot their stones, the ballistas shot their arrows along with the archers who had lined themselves up down in the bailey.

The arrows rained on the Ortaks, who were having a hard time defending themselves by now, as the stones from the catapults took a heavy toll.

Meanwhile, the Ortaks were lining themselves up at the West side of the castle, getting ready to attack from that side.

Captain Harleff had prepared for this as well, and now he sent his archers to the West wall, where they lined themselves up along with oil and fat to pour on the attackers. The best archers were placed at the bastions, where they had more chance to get a clean shot at the attackers if they reached the wall.

Now the overhang on the castle wall will come in handy when they attack, Duke John thought as he watched over his castle from the windows of the castle tower.

The main battle was still at the front gate, as the Ortaks loaded their war machines while trying to shield themselves from the arrows and the stones that continued raining down on them, killing and wounding many. Down in the valley, many had been assigned the task of rebuilding the siege tower for another raid at the castle.

Captain Harleff had stepped down from the wall and into the yard, to give his men at the war machines orders when he heard the horn sounding. The Ortaks were in place to attack the West side. He looked that way and saw his men preparing themselves with the pots of oil and fat, getting ready to pour it over the attackers as they approached.

Almost at the same time, a loud, thundering noise sounded as the first stone from an Ortak war machine landed on the uplifted drawbridge.

He was startled by the loud explosion, but he was quick to recover. He knew that the drawbridge would hold for a long time before it gave in, then there were the thick, heavy doors inside, which could also take a lot of beating before that would give in. Inside of that was the portcullis, so the Ortaks had a massive obstacle in front of them, before breaking into this castle.

His men adjusted the war machines under his orders, and then launched their next line of missiles, landing on the attacking forces outside.

Then the captain looked to the East wall, where he saw that the archers at the bastions had started shooting their arrows. He ran up the staircase to the eastern wall, to get a better view of what was going on there. He saw that the archers, mostly old men, were shooting down from the bastions on that side of the wall.

He ran to the nearest bastion and saw several Ortaks soldiers out of uniform and armour, who were trying to climb the wall. Fortunately, his archers had been able to shoot them all down, so far.

Now he looked at the Northside to see a large group of

arrows from the Ortaks as they raised up into the air at the same time his guards stationed on the wall sounded the warning sound of their horn. His men down below, inside the bailey, covered themselves with their shields, blocking the arrows that rained down on them.

He ran to the Southside to see that the Ortaks were climbing the cliff leading up to the castle, and the archers at the bastions were shooting them down.

The Ortaks were attacking the castle from all sides now, but his archers and the brave men by the war machines stood their ground in defence of their castle. He ran back to the West side of the wall, where he saw a large number of Ortaks attacking from that side, crossing the rough terrain, shielding themselves from the arrows coming from the wall, and trying to raise their ladders against the wall. Some of them had managed to get their ladders in place and had started climbing.

As he had instructed his men, they now poured the oil on the ladders below, and from the bastions where the archers had a good overview of the wall, they were able to attack the ladders with flaming arrows. Their attempt to attack the Westside failed, and they found themselves trapped by the wall in large numbers, where the archers kept shooting at them, leaving no escape.

The Ortaks answered by shooting arrows themselves, but with little result. The guard quickly covered themselves, when a storm of arrows rained down on them. Their attempt to defeat Castor Castle had failed, and it was obvious there was no hope of success by the end of that same day. The horn sounded, and slowly, the Ortaks removed themselves away from the castle, taking the wounded with them, leaving behind the bodies of the dead.

That evening the people at the castle smiled in their relief, celebrating the success they had gained. They had survived the attack from the Ortaks, and at least three hundred Ortaks lay dead outside the castle.

However, the Ortaks had placed many good archers on the ground during the battle, and there were some casualties within the castle as well. The Ortaks had shot at the guards stationed atop the castle wall, and thirty of their own men lay wounded or dead.

The people of the castle realised that this was probably the first day of many. The Ortaks would not give in so easily. They would have to prepare their defence again. Even so, they were able to rest that night, and most of them slept well, by the campfires that they kept burning in the bailey. The women and the children who had been kept inside the castle during the day of the attack, out of harm's way, came out now, to attend to the wounded and to be with their loved ones who had been part of the fight.

All was quiet that night. The guards on the wall looked down into the valley, where the Ortaks' campfires lit up the whole valley, like some unreal image of what they were used to seeing from the castle wall.

Sounds coming down from the Northside of the valley, from hammering and sawing, reached their ears throughout the entire night, until daybreak, when all went quiet again.

The next day started just like the day before. The castle guard heard the horn as it was sounded down in the valley, and then the sound of the siege tower reached them as it made its way up the road toward the gate.

But there was no morning mist now, so as soon as the sun came up, the castle guard had a good view over the whole terrain, and what they saw this time was quite scary.

Down by the road, the Ortaks had lined up not one, but three siege towers, one after another in a row, and they stood there waiting to be pushed up the road toward the castle.

The guard woke up those who were still asleep, after standing late watch up on the wall during the night, and they ran to their posts. The battle would soon begin again.

The Ortaks made the same attempt as they had the day before, dragging the siege towers to the gate. And like the day before, the trebuchets launched their stones as soon as their enemies had reached the right spot, and as the day before, the first siege tower was smashed all over the place, as five of the stones hit their mark.

Then the castle guard saw the Ortaks went off the road and headed to the Westside, and like the day before, they kept themselves out of range of the castle's war machines and arrows.

Only this time, there was something different about their tactics. They were carrying something with them. At the same time, another siege tower was being pushed up the road approaching from the North. The trebuchets had been reloaded and were ready to relaunch their stones, at the same time the second siege tower reached the marked spot on the road. The trebuchets launched their stones, but only one of the six missiles hit their mark. And the siege tower gained ground, moving closer and closer, not having been damaged enough to be stopped.

Captain Harleff realised that when the trebuchets launched their missiles, as heavy as the stones were, there would always be a chance that they would move or slide a bit to the side, forcing them to readjust the angle with each launch to be on target for the same spot they had marked off.

They had overlooked that, as the Ortaks had hoped they

would. This is why the Ortaks were approaching the castle with three towers in a row. They were hoping that they would get one tower up to the castle if the Castle did not have the opportunity to regroup and think out their defence. One tower was all they would need to attack; destroying the other two would be no considerable blow.

Seeing the siege tower approaching undamaged, the captain called out in fright and anger to the men at the catapults. They had loaded their machines, and stood there by them, waiting for his signal.

The siege tower was approaching uncomfortably fast when he gave the catapults the signal of shooting, but at the same time, a storm of arrows rose up in the air from the ranks of the Ortaks, and the sound of the guard's horn pierced the air in a warning.

The captain and his men had barely enough time to raise their shields to cover themselves from the arrows. When the stones from the catapults rained on the siege tower, it was smashed down to the ground, obliterated and reduced to small pieces. At the exact same time, though, the third siege tower was reaching the aiming point for the trebuchets.

Only three trebuchets had been reset for aim when the captain gave the signal to launch. He watched as the stones sailed through the air, but this time they missed just by an inch. One of the rocks even touched the tower as it passed by, and he had to stifle a groan at the waste.

The tower came at them with more haste than he had seen before. It was for sure that they had in mind to get this tower all the way, no matter what. When it had only a few metres to go, they had started lowering the landing bridge. As the captain gave the order to relaunch the catapults, he heard hammering sounds coming from the West wall.

He looked in that direction and saw stones coming over the wall and hitting the bastion, but not with any significant results. The walls and the bastions of this castle were five metres thick, and it would take more than catapults to break them down.

The castle's catapults threw their stones at the tower, and for a brief moment, his chest tightened with fear as he thought the siege tower would last through the attack. Then one of the stones that had landed high on the tower dropped down, falling on one of the four wheels and breaking it to pieces.

The tower listed to one side. The Ortaks had managed to place the tower's landing bridge across the ditch in front of the castle gate, and the Ortaks came running from the tower, crossing the bridge and onto the wall.

But then the tower with only three wheels lost its balance and, with a terrible racket, it fell into the ditch.

The attacking Ortaks met a massive storm of arrows as they came running out from the siege tower, and most of them were killed on the spot. But even so, five managed to run across onto the castle wall.

Still more came running out from the siege tower, trying to cross the bridge, but were shot down by archers at the bastions on both sides. The Ortaks who managed to cross fought bravely, but eventually, they were all killed by the guards, but not before they had managed to strike down six men of the castle guard.

Another storm of arrows went through the air, and once more, the castle guard covered themselves. The attempt to attack the North wall at the gate had failed once again, but the attack on the West wall was still raging.

The captain hurried over to the bastion at the West

corner of the wall to take a look at the situation. He saw where the Ortaks had lined up five catapults and placed them between the large rocks. They were trying to create a foundation for what seemed to be a trebuchet.

That can never happen, he thought, then he ran down the wall into the bailey, to his men stationed at the two trebuchets closest to the West wall. He gave them an order to place the trebuchet at the West wall, aiming at the catapults, but instructed they first destroy the construction of the trebuchet.

Then the warning sound of an arrow storm sounded, and they all took cover. While his men were dragging the trebuchets and lining them up at the West wall, the captain ran to the East wall, to find his archers at the bastions. They informed him there had been attempts to climb up, but not as many as the day before.

He had not given an order for an arrow storm since he wanted to save the arrows for as long as he could. Instead, his archer had been instructed to find the weak spot and make every shot count. He had young lads helping out by picking up the enemy arrows as they were shot over the wall and bringing water to his men.

He placed himself in one of the bastions at the Westside, where he had a good view of the Ortaks. He was trying to estimate what they would do if they attacked. His men had now dragged the huge trebuchets to their places with the help of fifteen horses and were filling up the heavy weight, trying to estimate how much they would need.

They had many years of experience with this, so he was fully confident that they would succeed in breaking down the enemy war machines. As he looked to the North side of the wall, over the gate, he saw his archers busy shooting over the wall, and an occasional arrow from the enemy flew over the wall and into the bailey.

His men at the trebuchets were now ready to launch again, and they had placed one man up on the wall, who gave them the signal where to aim. Each of them looked at him, waiting for his orders. The captain nodded, and the two trebuchets launched their first missiles.

His eyes followed the rocks as they reached their highest points, then they landed, and one of them smashed directly into a catapult, breaking it down between the rock on each side of it, and the men standing beside it were thrown aside.

The other stone landed about one metre to the right, straight on top of two men beside the catapult. The captain was pleased. The Ortaks were learning that they could not defeat their castle, and they were learning the hard way.

That day passed, and by nightfall, the two trebuchets at the West side had broken down every war machine the Ortaks had raised, and the Ortaks had left their posts. They headed for their camp down in the valley when the sound of the horn was heard.

The captain stood up on the wall and watched them as they left, once again pleased with how the day had gone.

They sheltered themselves as they approached the castle to pick up their comrades who had been wounded. Bodies littered the ground, and pieces of the siege towers were scattered all over the ramp and down in the ditch.

But all went quiet as the dark of the night set in, and once more, the castle guard saw where the lights from the Ortaks' campfires brightened up the valley below.

Captain Harleff stood staring down into the valley, planning what else there was to be done if the Ortaks attacked the next morning again. He had only four trebuchets guarding the main gate now, but he did not expect the Ortaks to use the same methods again, as it had not worked well for them so far.

But then, what?

His men had estimated that they had either killed or wounded more than nine hundred Ortaks in the two days of their attacks. But there were thirty men of the castle guard, that lay wounded, and fifteen had been killed.

As the captain stood there, his thoughts raging ahead, one of the castle guards approached him.

"The duke calls for you, Captain," the man said.

The captain nodded and headed down the stairs leading into the bailey. As he entered the keep, he saw the wounded men being attended to in a big room that used to be one of the quarters of the castle guard. He stopped there for a while to let the men see him, and he nodded his approval at them.

The keep was full of people from the villages down in the valley. He saw the fright in their eyes as he passed them on his way to meet the duke.

He entered the main hall, and the duke was sitting in his chair, waiting for him. He bowed before his master.

"You have done well, Captain," said the duke in a low, shaky voice.

"Thank you, my lord. I have good men with me, as His Lordship knows."

The Duke nodded. "Yes, you have, and you are not taking all the credit, as usual," said the duke, as a small, brief grin was seen crossing his lips, but it was only for a moment. It was evident that he was not in a joyful spirit, scared even.

"How long do you think we can stand against the Ortaks like this?" His eyes almost pleaded with the captain.

"That I cannot answer, my lord. We have been able to

break down their siege towers so far. We still have enough stones to last us for two more days. We have a large storage of bows and arrows, so we are well equipped for now, but I don't know how long they will attack. We have no choice other than to just wait and see."

The duke sat there thinking for a while, staring down at the floor, then he looked at the captain again.

"You are aware that we will get no reinforcement from the king. We are, in fact, alone in this battle," he said in a low voice, trying to keep this from being heard by others inside the castle.

"I am well aware of that, my lord," answered the captain. "We still have the upper hand in this battle, and we are not about to give up." The captain straightened himself in front of his master.

"I am glad to hear that, Captain. You may leave now, as you need your rest for tomorrow. It is comforting for the people at the castle and me to know we can rely on your courage." Captain Harleff bowed his head before his master and left.

He headed out of the keep and up to the wall, the words of his master weighing on him. Being reminded of how much was at stake had a great impact on him. It gave him more hope. He did not stop until he stood at the top of the Barbican. He stood there beside the guard to watch for a while, staring out into the darkness.

"Did you stand guard last night?" he suddenly asked the guard without looking at him.

"Yes, Captain." The guard was obviously startled by the question.

"What is different now, from yesterday, Soldier?" The captain's voice showed a little excitement.

"What do you mean by different, sir?" the guard asked, feeling uneasy.

"Listen, man, what do you hear?" The captain was more excited now.

"I hear nothing, sir," replied the guard.

"Exactly! There is no hammering! There is no wood-sawing! All is quiet! They are not building siege towers anymore."

"What does that mean, sir?" The guard was still not sure what was expected of him.

"That I do not know, my good man, but we will not be seeing siege towers attacking us in the morning, that is one thing I do know," said the captain, looking out and down to the valley.

To COMMAND the attacks on Castor Castle, Commander Triskar had placed himself upon a large rock overlooking the area at the North-west end of the castle. From there, he had a good overview of the area and kept his horn blowers and two commanding officers at his side to assist him.

On the first day, he watched how the castle guard managed to break down the siege tower, even while it still had almost one hundred metres to go before it reached the wall.

The Westside was nearly invincible. He knew before they even started that without an army four or five times larger than their current forces, they would not even stand a chance.

He was quite well prepared for this siege, as his men took ten wagons of equipment with them from White River.

Wood for four siege towers, five catapults, ten ballistas, and three trebuchets were waiting to be used, in case he should find ground flat enough for them to stand on.

So at the end of the first day, he had his men build three siege towers instead of one, hoping they might have a chance of getting at least one of them to the castle wall.

He had only enough wood for those three left. If he wanted to build more, it would take time. He would have to send his men out into the woods to chop trees.

He was more optimistic the second day, and when he saw that they had managed to get the last siege tower to the castle wall, he grinned. But then the tower fell down into the ditch, and his men were slaughtered by the castle's archers as they tried to cover themselves. And finally, when he saw them targeting the war machines at the Westside, he realised that this battle was lost for him and his men.

He returned to the valley with his men, angry and hurt. He had just been defeated, which was something that he had never had to deal with before as a commanding officer in the Ortaks Army.

He passed the wounded soldiers, as he made his way to his horse that had been kept for him by his servant. He mounted, then rode down the valley all the way to his tent.

He dismounted without speaking to anyone. He gave his guard the order that he was not to be disturbed.

He poured himself a glass of wine and sat there in the dark, thinking.

The next morning his commanding officers stood outside his tent, waiting for their orders. He raised his head and looked at the castle, bathed in the morning sun, as it rose above the landscape. Then he turned his attention to his men.

"How many have we lost in the last two days?"

They looked worriedly at each other, then one of them spoke.

"We lost four hundred and fifty men, and there are about the same number wounded and unable to fight, Commander," he said.

The commander stood there in silence for a while before he spoke again, quietly. "We need to collect the bodies of those who are lying by the castle walls and bury them. They should have a decent burial."

The officers looked at each other. They realised that they were not to attack the castle that day, but they kept quiet.

The commander asked for his horse, then he gave his men their orders for the day.

As he rode towards the castle, he saw his men standing quietly, looking at him. He knew they were waiting for an opportunity to collect their comrades' corpses so that they could bury them.

Commander Triskar knew if he approached the castle alone, they would not harm him. He was no threat to them, and it was in their best interest to listen to him and hear what he had to say.

He stopped out of reach from the archers and called out.

"Permission to approach." He waited for a while, then a voice from the castle wall called back.

"Permission granted."

Carefully, he approached the castle, stopping when he was about thirty metres from the ditch, to call out again, though not as loud as before.

"I am Triskar, commander in the Ortaks Army. I seek permission to bring the bodies of my men to my camp, so we can give them a decent burial." The commander waited for an answer, and after a few minutes, a voice called out from the wall.

"I am Captain Harleff, head of the castle defence. Your permission is granted, on conditions."

"What conditions?" Commander Triskar was beginning to be sceptical.

"There will be no more than ten men at a time at the castle wall. They will be unarmed, and without any armour."

Commander Triskar nodded. "I accept your conditions," he said, then he rode off.

The rest of the day, and the next, his men worked on fetching their comrades, using the wagons they had brought with them to carry equipment from White River.

The castle guard kept a good eye on them, but all went well.

Commander Triskar had not received any word from his general, and with no reinforcement, he decided to abandon the castle siege. After burying the fallen soldiers, he headed out with twelve hundred men to strengthen his forces at White River, leaving only eight hundred men at Castor Castle.

He knew if the castle guard tried to engage his men in a battle on even ground, his men would prevail.

Duke John and his guards watched as the commander and his men left. They knew they were still trapped inside the castle, and their only hope was if the king decided to send his army to break the Ortaks' siege.

As Commander Triskar reached the hill, where he had seen Castor Castle for the first time, he turned to have a final look. The castle stood there, undefeated, proudly rising towards the sky on that cold autumn day.

It was beginning to snow, and he could see that the

mountain in the background was covered with a grey blanket, as the first snow of winter had fallen on it during the night before.

He turned his horse again and continued his journey. He had the feeling he would not see that castle again.

9 REVENGE AT EASEL CASTLE

*R*ebuilding Crown Castle did not take long. Most of it was woodwork, and Sir William had a good crew of workers who were experienced in stone and wood-working, and they raised the wall and the houses within the first three weeks.

Sir Alfred led a patrol group that kept watch for outlaws, and there were always soldiers garrisoned at the castle at all times. Things were getting back to normal again.

Or so it seemed on the surface. Sir William's memory of the Ortaks attack and the Vargs upon the Heath, were still haunting him in his sleep. Still, he often found himself looking over the Heath, expecting their return.

The winter was not as hard as he had experienced on the Heath many times in the past, but it was cold enough to create more pain in his leg than he cared for. But all winters pass, and with spring comes more sun, longer days, and less frost. Sir William regained his good mood with the change of seasons.

One spring day a group of riders arrived from Borg Castle. They had come by order from the queen. Their mission was to mark the route between Crown Castle and Top Valley, which they had already done, so the army could build a road.

Another route was to be laid from Crown Castle to Peak Castle for the same purpose. Sir William was given his orders too. To rebuild the path leading from Crown Castle to Storm Castle, to create a safer passing between the two.

There was only one road across the Heath at this time, the road between Bridge Village and Peak Castle, leaving all that land untamed. And the path between Storm Castle and Crown Castle was in a bad state, to say the least.

The Heath was a great, vast land in the northern part of Eniktronia, with hills, woodlands, mountains, pastures, and swamps. It was only possible for a few people to cross.

The Heath was dangerous territory, swarming with wolves, bears, wild Boars, and a vast range of birds, wildlife, and game. There were lakes, rivers, and streams. Sir William had always found the Heath to be a beautiful place to be in during the summers, but they were hard lands in the winter season.

Having more roads would mean safer crossing over the Heath, for the soldiers, travellers, and merchants.

The group from Borg Castle contained thirty men, mostly soldiers, but also hunters, who knew the Heath well and were able to guide them across.

But there were two men amongst them, who stirred a curiosity for Sir William, Gils from Peak Castle and Asgrim from Borg Castle. They had been sent by their masters, but the reason why they would have been chosen seemed unclear. Sir William did not have to speak to the two for long, to wonder why they had been sent on this mission.

One of them was a wanderer from Antonia, and the other was a ferryman on Lake Etu. Sir William had met many odd people in his lifetime, and he found the two of them very strange indeed. He learned, however, that they were in a personal acquaintance to the queen, and friends to His Lordship. Peculiar acquaintance, he thought.

But, not for me to judge their masters, he thought as the group left the castle the next morning, heading north to find the safest route to Peak Castle.

Leading the group was Lieutenant Larus, a strong, hard-headed man, who kept good discipline within his men. And like Sir William, it was a puzzle to him why the two had been placed in his group as if it was not hard enough to have hunters, who were not used to a soldier's life. But he had to find a route between Crown Castle and Peak Castle that would not take more than two days to travel by foot, and three days for a wagon.

By the evening they were camped by a small river that ran between two high, grassy hills. They had good pastures for their horses on the other side of the stream, and a shelter from the cold early spring wind, coming from the North.

They slept well that night. As they woke up the next morning, they found that fog had crept over the Heath during the night, so thick they hardly saw their horses on the other side of the stream.

They ate breakfast, and Gils crossed the creek to fetch his horse and Asgrim's. He had tied their horses a bit farther downstream, where he thought they had better grass for grazing.

When he came back to the campsite across the stream,

the soldiers had already saddled their horses and were ready to head off. Gils handed Asgrim the reins of his horse, and they started to saddle them.

"We will head upstream. You two can catch up with us when we take a rest." Lieutenant Larus looked down on them from his horse, obviously unhappy with the delay, but he said nothing else, just looked at them as they lifted their saddles onto their horses' backs. Then he turned to his men, and Asgrim and Gils watched them as they vanished into the fog.

"Why did you have to pasture the horses so far away?" Asgrim was unhappy with his fellow traveller.

"The horses had better grass there," replied Gils as he tightened the girth.

"They had no time to wait for us," Asgrim almost cried.

"We will catch up with them as the lieutenant said." Gils hoisted himself up on his horse. Then he waited until Asgrim was in his saddle. It took a while since Asgrim was not a flexible man when it came to mounting his horse. When he finally managed to settle in his saddle, they rode after the others.

There was minimal visibility; the hills seemed higher, the trees taller, as they could not see the treetops as they passed them. After about an hour of riding, they reached a curve in the river, where they stopped. They had lost the tracks of the others some time ago, not realising it until now.

They tried to look, to see if there were any marks, thinking perhaps they could spot some hoof prints on the solid ground by the river, but there was nothing, just rocks. They saw some moist moss a bit farther from the bank, but still no signs or footprints of the soldiers passing there.

"What now? You have gotten us lost." Asgrim looked around, confused and frightened.

"He said that they would head upstream, so we will just do the same. We are bound to run into them if we do," replied Gils, acting as if he did not hear what Asgrim had said. They continued their journey.

Riding through the thick fog, they tried to see what was ahead, moving slowly but steadily.

They continued moving farther upstream, until, about four hours later, they found themselves trapped in a canyon, between two rocky hills, and they had to stop.

There was no way to go any farther, as the area ahead was blocked. The river had turned into rapids coming out from the canyon. They tried but weren't able to see into the canyon.

A fine drizzle hit their faces, and a thundering noise ahead told them that there was a waterfall inside. Gils had been riding in front the whole time, and now he turned in his saddle and looked at Asgrim with questioning eyes.

"I think I saw a crossing farther downstream," said Asgrim, in a loud voice, trying to be heard over the river.

"Why should we cross the river?" asked Gils, trying to come up with some answer of why they were lost.

"They may have done so at some point, and we may have overlooked that possibility," answered Asgrim, the fright in his voice growing stronger.

Gils sat there, thinking for a while without saying anything. The fog was even thicker than before, or so it seemed. He had no idea where he was, or in what direction he was going. He looked around one more time, then turned to Asgrim and nodded.

They went back the same way they came, and about two

hours later, they came to a spot where the river was wider and made a good crossing.

Without any hesitation, they rode into the river, and as they came upon the other bank, they turned right and followed the river, or so they thought. This time, they followed a narrow path that led them into a wooded area, but they thought they heard the river close by, so they kept on following the path.

About two hours later, they decided to take a rest. With no sunshine, they had no idea what time of the day it was, but they were getting tired, and as they entered a clearing in the woods, they stopped the horses and dismounted. They had some food in their saddlebags, and they took a minute to eat.

"Do you have any idea where we are?" asked Asgrim as he put the rest of his food back into his saddlebag.

"No, not exactly. All I know is that we have to follow the river upstream," said Gils and sniffed.

"I thought you had given up on that sniffing." Asgrim was a bit annoyed to hear the habit return.

"I do what I want." Gils sniffed again.

"I think we have gone too far from the river." Asgrim acted like he didn't hear the latest remark from Gils.

"Well, it's over there." Gils nodded his head in the direction he thought the river to be in, then he mounted his horse again. "We still have some daylight left, and we can't dwell here for too long if we are to catch up with the others." He waited for Asgrim while he mounted his horse.

As they were about to head off again, they heard a strange noise, coming from the left of them. It was a loud, roaring noise like something was being dragged on the ground.

Their horses whinnied, and they suddenly darted off, moving away from the noise as fast as they possibly could.

Asgrim screamed out, and, like Gils, he grabbed the saddle and held on as hard as he could, trying not to fall off.

Their horses carried them off at high speed, far away from whatever it was that made the noise, and as fast as their feet could possibly carry them.

This all happened so fast that they had no time to see or figure out where the horses were going. They just ran farther and farther away, crossing pastures, streams, through woodlands, and across rough terrains. They had no idea how long the horses ran, but they did not stop until they were too tired to run any farther.

Their riders were tired from riding them, as well, and when they finally stopped in a green, hilly pasture, at least two hours later, the men both shivered from head to toe with fear and excitement as they dismounted.

"What was that?" screamed Asgrim as he stepped down, his eyes wide in his reddened face.

"I don't know, but whatever it was, I am glad we had mounted our horses before it came at us," replied Gils and bent over, his hands bracing against his thighs. "My legs are done in. I have never ridden a horse that fast before, and for so long," he mumbled, then he sniffed and stretched himself out, pushing on the small of his back with his hands. "I am all beaten up," he mumbled again.

There was a large rock in the middle of the pasture where the horses had stopped, and there were some bushes and a few trees close by. They strolled over to the rock, looking around, to see if there was any more threat in the area. Their hearts were beating very fast. The thought of that awful thing they had heard was still fresh in their minds.

The horses were still terrified and shivering too, and sweating. They unsaddled them and tied them to a bush near the rock. They patted them slowly, hoping they would calm down so they could get some rest.

The fog was starting to clear up; it was not as thick as before. Now they could at least somewhat see the surrounding area and the hills. They saw that they were in a green pasture, with hills and woodlands nearby.

They finally saw some sunlight and realised that the day was almost over, so they decided to make camp there by the rock for the night.

A perfect place to camp, thought Gils as he started to gather some firewood for the campfire.

"Can you hear this?" Asgrim half-whispered. Gils was in the middle of gathering the firewood a few metres away and stopped and raised himself up, listening.

"What? What am I listening to?" He sniffed.

"Exactly! It is all quiet, there are no sounds at all, not even a bird." Asgrim was getting worked up as he whispered, looking at Gils in terror. Gils stood there with the firewood in his hands, also frightened as he realised Asgrim was right.

"You are scaring me," Gils said in a high-pitched voice, almost wetting his pants.

"Don't talk so loud. Someone might hear you," Asgrim said fiercely as he took a few steps closer to Gils.

"Like who? There is no one around, you just said that. Will you make up your mind before I shit myself?" said Gils, looking around to see if there was anyone else in sight. There was no one to be seen.

They stood there for a moment, listening and looking around, frightened and confused, then Gils pulled himself together and started to make a fire.

"Are you out of your mind?" Asgrim whispered, red in the face, looking as if he had just seen a ghost.

"What did I do now?" Gils replied, whispering this time.

"You are making a fire, you idiot," Asgrim almost called out, and he waved his hands. "They can see the smoke for miles."

Gils was confused, looking from Asgrim to the fire he just made, thinking.

"But that would mean that Lieutenant Larus can see it too," he said as if he was convincing himself the fire was a good idea.

Asgrim said nothing, but waved his hands again, and started pacing around the fire, and looking around as if he was expecting someone to pop up at any moment.

However, the darkness was looming in, and within a few minutes, it was pitch-black. Then, finally, Asgrim stopped pacing. He knew Gils was right; there was a small chance that they could be seen by Larus and his men. He finally calmed down enough to sit beside Gils next to the fire.

They sat there quietly staring into the flames and warming themselves. They both realised how tired they really were, as the fire had soothed them, and finally, they both lay down to sleep.

How long they slept, no one knows, but they woke up to the same roaring noise they heard the day before. They both pulled themselves to their feet, every muscle hurting from head to toe.

The sleepiness cleared in a hurry when they heard their horses whinnying and thrashing against the bush where they had tied them the night before.

Suddenly, their horses ran past them, so close they almost

knocked them down. Then they heard the roaring noise again, this time closer.

Whatever this thing was, it was coming at them at high speed.

Asgrim screamed and started running after the horses with Gils on his tail. They had no weapons, only their knives, so to stand and fight was not an option. The fog had cleared up, and there was a bright moonlight that helped them to see where they were going.

They lost sight of the horses after running for a few minutes, but a high cliff rose up in front of them, and they headed that way without thinking.

They came to a small stream they had to cross on their way. Without any hesitation, Asgrim ran into the stream, but it was deeper than it seemed, and he suddenly fell face-first, landing on his stomach in the ice-cold water.

Gils managed to stay on his feet, and grabbed Asgrim by the hand, dragging him back to his feet. As they reached the other bank, they heard whatever it was coming after them as it roared, and Asgrim screamed again.

Gils stopped for a brief moment to turn his head, desperate to see how close the creature following them was.

He saw a large, black shadow of some sort coming over the pastures. Due to the darkness, he could not see the beast clear enough, but it seemed to have small feet and a tail, and it was running fast.

Unconsciously, he made some sort of a noise that sounded like a scream, then he kept on running, following Asgrim, now racing up the slope to the cliff.

Using both hands and feet, they scrambled up the steep slope and all the way to the cliff. Asgrim started climbing, but, out of breath and without any energy left in his body, he just stopped, and so did Gils.

They had nowhere to go, and the beast had now crossed the stream and was making its way up the slope. That beast was not slowing down.

Once more, Asgrim screamed, and they drew their knives, waiting for the attack.

Then, all of a sudden, a light burst out, and all was bright as day. Then they saw the beast for the first time. It was a huge animal of some sort.

They had never seen anything like it before. It had a big mouth, and its teeth were big and sharp as knives. With a long body that ended in a long tail, it was coming at them, darting up the slope.

When the whole area went bright as sunlight, the beast stopped and made a horrible roaring sound. It seemed to have been blinded by the light. It shook its head and again made a horrible sound. They just stood there, paralysed with fear. They had no idea what was going on, or where the light came from.

Then that horrible beast started to back down the slope again. Still roaring, it backed farther and farther away, moving slowly.

Then a large arrow or a bolt hit the beast in the left side, and it turned to face its attacker, just as a large number of bolts came from the other direction. With a horrible roar, it rolled onto its back, dead.

Asgrim and Gils just stood there, unable to believe what they had just seen. They had never seen or heard of a creature like that, and they couldn't seem to stop staring at it. Then they heard a voice coming from their right.

"Gils, are you all right, my friend?" It was a woman.

Gils was not a brave man, and he was afraid to look to see who was talking to him. It was Asgrim, standing on his left, who bent a bit so he could see who it was. He straightened himself up again. Then, after a moment, Gils turned his head, and beside him, only two metres away, stood a woman.

A very beautiful woman, wearing a long, blue silk dress and golden shoes. Her dark, greying hair lay down her back, and she was holding a short wand. At the end of that wand was some sort of a stone or a rock, which is what was making the bright light. Gils quickly turned his head again to notice that the beast had vanished. Where did it go? He thought, mystified.

"She knows you, Gils," Asgrim whispered.

"I don't think so," Gils whispered back.

"Gils does not remember me." The woman smiled as she lowered the wand and placed the other hand on the stone at the end, decreasing the light to the size of a small campfire. "We use to play together as children on Duck Island, but that was long ago." She kept looking at Gils.

"I like your dress," Asgrim said, trying to ease the awkward moment, because Gils was not replying, just staring down the slope in front of him.

"I did recognise you, Antea, just could not believe you were here," he finally mumbled, then he sniffed, after which an awkward silence settled over them once again.

"So, Antea, is it?" Asgrim tried to smile. "Are you from Duck Island, then?" Asgrim gave Gils a nudge. "I am Asgrim, by the way, and I am so glad to see you," he added, but Gils was just staring in silence.

"Nice to make your acquaintance," Asgrim added, still smiling.

"It is nice to meet you too, Asgrim. Gils has always been a shy man. We must give him some time," she said, and then she turned and gave some sort of signal to her right side, and a few moments later they heard horses below the slope. The woman turned to them again.

"You will find your horses down in the pastures. You should go back to where you camped for the night and wait there for your fellow travellers. They will find you if you stay put," she said, and her smile was gone. Then she placed her hand on the wand, and the light was turned off.

They stood there for a while, trying to comprehend what had just happened, and what the woman had just said, then Asgrim broke the silence.

"We should get back." He started to make his way down the slope, trying not to fall. Gils followed him, and then they headed out for the stream they had crossed earlier.

It took them some time to get used to the dark again, but they found the horses, calmed down and tied to a bush on the other side of the stream.

They made it to their campsite, and again, Gils started a fire, and by the time he was finished, the sun was up. They sat there staring into the flames for a long time, then Asgrim looked at his fellow traveller.

"Who is Antea, Gils? Is she an Elf?"

"Yes, she is an Elf," Gils said and nodded as he added some firewood.

"Who do you think killed that beast, Gils? Elves?" Asgrim was excited and a bit scared.

"Probably." Gils did not take his eyes from the fire. The shock he felt after seeing Antea after all these years was even greater than seeing that horrible beast.

"Then she and that beast just disappeared, as they had

never been," said Asgrim as if to himself. "I think it's best if we just keep quiet about this, don't you think?" He looked around to see if there was anyone there. "No one will ever believe us anyway. They will only make fun at us," he whispered and started to look into the fire, like Gils.

Gils nodded. No one would ever believe what they had just experienced.

They sat there most of the day and did as the Elven woman had asked of them, staying by the campsite.

It was almost evening, and the shadows were getting longer when they saw someone approaching on the other side of the pasture. When they got closer, they recognised Lieutenant Larus and his men. He stopped his horse in front of them. He sat there for a while, then he dismounted, looking at them without saying a word, but they could clearly see the dislike in his frowning face.

"We will stay here for the night and head off tomorrow morning," he told his men. Then he unsaddled his horse.

Neither the lieutenant nor his men spoke to them or asked what had happened to them. After having an early breakfast, they all headed off for Peak Castle the next morning.

It was not until much later that Gils was told that the lieutenant and his men had reached Peak Castle without them, and were given orders to return to the Heath to find them, or accept being punished for leaving His Lordship's friend and a friend to the queen, as well as the royal ferryman, alone upon the Heath.

QUEEN EGNY FACED hectic times that winter at Kings Rock,

after reclaiming her kingdom. Not only did she have to work to regain her people's loyalty in Otanga, but also at restoring law and order throughout her kingdoms, which now numbered three.

She had sent Sir Brian to Hunting Valleys as her representative in early autumn and received reports from him throughout the winter informing her of the harbour and the town it had created in Troll Fjord.

And by spring, she sent him two hundred men, as she had promised him. They were to get rid of those outlaws in King Forest, led by a man named Lukas, who was getting quite annoying, to say the least.

However, not a word had been heard from him for some time now, and she was beginning to worry.

She had sent most of her army to Eniktronia, not needing them all at Kings Rock. Most of them had orders to return to Eniktronia Castle, but some of them were sent to Peak Castle and Borg Castle.

She wanted to have them close by if she was to summon the army to cross Bending Pass to Antonia. They were delivering orders to Lord Klaus, and Commander Agnar, for their administration.

Amongst those orders were instructions to build more roads, especially in the most remote areas, like the Heath and the western part of Eniktronia.

With Axel by her side at Kings Rock that winter, she held a meeting with her advisers on all matters of state. One day in late autumn, when she had been at her throne, receiving the news from Hergia of Vikings invading the lands north of Raven Rock, a messenger arrived, and she could see on his face that something was very wrong.

He was afraid to speak, knowing how bad this news was

and not wanting to be the one who had to deliver it. He bowed before his queen, then finally pulled himself together.

"I bear news from Kings Forest, Your Highness," he finally said, though he dared not look up from the floor. She sat there looking at him, silent, and frightened at the same time. "Sir Brian is dead, My Sovereign. He was ambushed by the outlaw they call Lukas. He killed most of our men, nearly two hundred and fifty of them." The messenger went silent, waiting for some reaction from his queen.

But she just sat there, quiet, pale, and distant. She was both angry and hurt. Sir Brian was not only her most reliable knight and ally, but also her personal friend. It was Sir Brian's work that had made her Queen of Otanga.

Axel was shocked as well, and when he saw the effect the news had on his queen, he gave the guards an order to remove the messenger from the hall and to guard him until he had a chance to interrogate him later. Then he ordered everyone out of the hall.

When they were all gone, his queen looked at him with questioning eyes but said nothing.

"I will deal with this. You do not have to worry about it," he said in a low, comforting voice. She nodded and stood up. Her maids came running to assist her and escorted her to her quarters.

When she was gone, Axel called for the messenger. That messenger was Sigurstein, who had been sent by Kristinn the lawman. Lord Axel sat down and asked him to explain what had happened.

And for the next two hours, he asked him about the ambush in every detail he could think of until he had all the information he needed. Then he sat there thinking for a minute before he ordered Sigurstein to get some rest.

He was to leave in haste the next morning for Troll Fjord with a message to Kristinn, the lawman. He asked the guards to summon the commanding officers who were from the area around Kings Forest and Lake Easel at the castle.

Lord Axel had little knowledge of Otanga, as his home-land was Serpenia. Now he would have to rely on those who were local.

After a long meeting with them, where he learned about the area and the landscape, he came to a conclusion. He sat down to write a letter to be delivered to Kristinn, the lawman.

Sigurstein left the castle the next morning in great haste, as he knew how important it was for him to reach Troll Fjord on time, for His Lordship's plan to work.

Axel called one of the officers and asked him to assemble fifty men. They were all to be from Otanga and should know the area well. And they were to be ready to ride with him within the next two days.

Axel was preparing for his journey later that day when he heard light footsteps by his door.

"What do you intend to do?" asked the queen as she stepped into his quarters. She knew Axel would not let the outlaw get away with killing Sir Brian; they had become too good of friends for that.

"I intend to eliminate the threat that your kingdom has of that outlaw. He has grown too strong. No longer can we withhold the laws in large part of the country, and the people know that" he replied, returning from the map on his table, and facing his queen.

"The tax collectors have been having a hard time collecting the taxes in the area west of Windbreak Moun-tains, and it is because of Lukas. His time will stop now," he added in a lower voice, and she took two steps closer to him, to have a better look into his eyes.

"And how will you accomplish that, my lord?" Her eyes were still looking intently at his, and she came even closer.

"I have sent Kristinn the lawman a letter, ordering him to summon our forces in Hunting Valleys. Then I gave him the order to approach the outlaws' camp from the West, but not before I have summoned Lukas to a meeting with me by the royal hunting castle at Lake Easel, to discuss a treaty," he said, without taking his eyes from hers.

He felt calm and content in her presence, and the smell of her skin almost made him smile, even in this moment of grief for their friend.

"What makes you think he will come to the meeting? And what kind of a treaty? I cannot remember having any intentions of making a treaty with that monster." He saw wrath in her eyes now.

"You don't have to worry about that, My Queen, no actual treaty will be made, but only you and I know that." He paused for a moment, to let the wrath within her eyes calm down again, and she almost smiled, he was sure of that. "You can trust me, My Queen. There will be no more outlaws taking over the laws in this country again when I'm finished with Lukas."

She nodded. "I trust you, like I always have, my lord." Now she did smile, but only for a brief moment. She turned and walked out of the room, leaving him alone with his thoughts.

Two days later Lord Axel left Kings Rock, heading for Lake Easel. Before he left, he sent another messenger, who was to go straight to Lukas in King Forest, bearing a letter summoning him to a small castle at the West side of Lake

Easel. The men in his company were from that area, and now, Lord Axel had to rely on their guidance for the success of this mission.

They rode the path that lay close to Windbreak Mountains. That meant deep valleys and high ridges. Lord Axel had never been in this part of the country before, but in some ways, it reminded him of the area in Serpenia, where he had spent his childhood, and later led his people to safety in Goat Valley.

Four days later they came upon a hill overlooking Lake Easel. It was just as his men had described it.

A beautiful lake in a green, fertile country, and in the far distance, on the West side of the lake, he saw the castle.

Easel Castle, as the people called it, had been built on a large rock out in the lake. It was almost an island, located at the end of a peninsula.

The road led them alongside the lake, through villages and farmlands, all the way to the peninsula, and ended by the castle drawbridge, which was about five metres over a moat created by the lake, and into the castle gate.

Lord Axel estimated that the peninsula was about two hundred metres long to the bridge, and fifty metres wide at the coast, tapering down to twenty metres at the end.

They crossed the bridge, where four men and two women greeted them inside the gate. They were elderly people, and as his men had told him, they were the castle keepers. They had been in the service of the late king for many years, and now offered their loyalty to their queen.

Lord Axel introduced himself to the castle staff, then he dismounted his horse, followed by his men, and the castle's keepers relieved them of their horses. Their mounts were brought to the stables, where they were unsaddled and given hay and water.

Axel looked around. Even though the castle was quite small, fifty men could defend it quite well, he thought, as he took the steps leading to the curtain wall.

The castle's staff had a meal ready for the newcomers. They had begun their preparations when they had seen them riding alongside the lake, approaching the castle. Lord Axel was carrying the royal coat of arms on a flag, and it could be seen from afar. A meat soup was always welcomed by Axel and his men.

After dining with his men, Axel sent ten of them into the woodlands, to the west of Kings Forest.

They were to scout and stand guard over the area. He had no intention of being caught by surprise by Lukas and his men.

He had estimated that Lukas would be arriving with his men two days from now. He had factored in how long it would take the messenger to reach him, and then Lukas having to gather his men, and march all the way to the castle.

There were no defensive machines at the castle since it was mainly used as a royal headquarters when the late king went on his hunting trips. But the high walls and lake and the surrounding area gave the castle an excellent defence.

All was quiet on the first day, and that allowed Lord Axel to meet some of the locals, and find out more about Lukas and his men. Early on the morning of the second day, his men returned to the castle, informing him Lukas had been seen arriving through the woods and was few hours behind them.

Lord Axel gave the order, and his men lifted the castle drawbridge, and then they waited.

By noon Lord Axel was standing on the castle wall along with his men when they saw the first outlaws approaching from the woodland and moving into the pastures.

At the same time, they saw in the distance, where the people of the villages fled east, alongside the lake and into the valleys above, the same way they had ridden through when they came from Kings Rock.

At first, it did not seem many were coming out of the woods, just a few scattered over a broad area.

About an hour later, though, Lord Axel decided those few must have been scouts because the pastures were suddenly packed with men, as they stormed out of the woodland all together. Axel and his men counted at least four hundred of them.

In a firm but slow steps, looking around the entire time, the outlaws came closer and closer, until they stopped at the shores where the peninsula began.

Then, one by one, they started to approach the castle, covering themselves behind their shields, until they reached the end of the road and the drawbridge landing. There, they stopped, since the drawbridge had been raised and they could not go any farther.

Many of them had no shields but covered themselves behind those who did.

Lord Axel noticed how well-armed they were, many of them appear to have formerly been soldiers, or perhaps they were carrying the weapons belonging to Sir Brian and his men, whom they had killed by the river such a short time ago.

Lord Axel clenched his fist at the thought. But then he

forced himself to calm down. His training as an archer came in handy now. He held his bow in his hand and waited for Lukas to approach.

No one from the front line seemed to be him. Then a man from the castle staff took a stand beside him, watching the outlaws as Lord Axel had requested he do.

"Do you see Lukas?" Axel whispered.

"Not yet, my lord, he is not here in the front." The man kept looking, then he whispered back, "He is in the middle, wearing a brown furry jacket, my lord." It took Axel only a few moments to spot him.

"You should go down now, old man. Things might get dangerous now," said Axel as he drew an arrow and placed it on his bow. The old man hurried down the stairs and into the keep, closing the door behind him.

"Any sign of our men?" Lord Axel asked the man next to him.

"No, my lord. Shouldn't they be here soon?" Lord Axel could hear the shivering fright in the man's voice.

"We must hope they will. Give them a few more hours."

By this time some of the outlaws in the front of the castle had started to wade into the water, to get across. Then another outlaw called out. It was a tall man, holding a big battle-axe and his shield in front of him.

"Lord Axel, I'm Lukas. Lower the bridge, so we can talk," he said and smiled.

In one quick move, Lord Axel lifted his bow and shot the man straight in the forehead. He fell face down into the water.

Five more arrows came from the castle wall, killing the men who had started wading into the water.

The outlaws raised their shields, to have a better cover,

and started to move backwards. Some of them even answered by shooting at the castle, but Axel and his men took cover.

Then one of Axel's men whispered, "They are here, my lord."

Lord Axel peeked over the castle wall and looked to the woodland. He saw what he had been waiting for.

Four thousand men, his soldiers from Hunting Valleys, led by Kristinn, the lawman, started coming out of the woodlands from all sides, surrounding the outlaws.

It took the outlaws some time to realise what had happened, and some of the men in the back rows started to make a run for it.

And as Lord Axel and his men watched from the castle wall, the outlaws did not get very far before they were shot down.

Then Lukas stepped out closer to the castle and called out.

"You wanted to make a treaty, Your Lordship." He held the letter in his hand.

"Yes, amongst other things, I did, but where is my messenger? My letter also stated that you should be led to this meeting by my messenger."

Lukas looked back at his men, who were now completely surrounded, then he turned his head to the castle again.

"We should hold this meeting, my lord." He received no response from the castle, and he knew he had to answer the question. After a short pause, he called out, "Your messenger is at my camp, Your Lordship."

"Your camp has now been burned down to the ground. Your livestock, along with your women and the children, are now being taken to Troll Fjord, and if my messenger has been hurt, you will be executed." Lukas realised now that it was all over for him; he had been led into a trap.

"Damn you!" he called out, and he had barely uttered the last word when Lord Axel's arrow went straight into his heart.

What happened next was well organised and carried out according to the orders Kristinn the lawman had received from Lord Axel.

The royal army moved in on the outlaws, who tried to fight back, but the army took their revenge for their comrades.

Outnumbered ten to one and trapped on the peninsula, the outlaws had no place to go. They fell by the swords, where they stood. Some dove into the lake, trying to swim away, only to be shot by the castle's archers.

Three hours later, all the outlaws had been killed, either in the fight or by execution.

The royal army stood in front of the castle, still holding their weapons when Lord Axel gave the order and his men lowered the castle drawbridge.

He stepped out onto the middle of the bridge and stopped there, still holding his bow in his hand, then he nodded to his men, and they fell on their knees and bowed before him.

Kristinn, the lawman, was a bit surprised. He knew most of his men from Hunting Valleys, and they had never bowed for anyone. Now they bowed before a man who had been a mere archer only two years earlier.

He did as his men and bowed, then, when they rose up again, he moved forward on the drawbridge and stopped in front of Lord Axel.

"Let me introduce myself. I am Kristinn, a lawman from Hunting Valleys," he said and bowed his head.

"I am glad to meet you, Kristinn. I am Axel, Lord of Erinstein, and I can see that you have received my letter, and brought me my army," he said, as he looked over Kristinn's shoulder at the men standing behind him.

"Yes, I did, and it surprised me how quickly they answered the call," he said, looking at the young men standing in front of him.

"Their loyalty to the queen is admirable, and they have been with us since we broke down the siege in Crown City." Lord Axel smiled.

"Their loyalty to the queen is unquestionable, but it is your leadership that they admire, Lord Axel," said Kristinn.

"We must clear this battleground and tend to the wounded, my good man, but we also must discuss other matters of state," said Lord Axel. He gave his men orders to see to the men who had been injured, then he turned to the castle again, this time followed by Kristinn, the lawman.

"What made you so certain that Lukas would show up here at the castle, my lord?" asked Kristinn as they walked into the main hall of the castle.

It was not much of a hall, more like a big room, where the late king had taken his meals with his fellow hunters. Inside the hall was a long dining table with benches on both sides, with a high-backed chair at the end.

It was here the king used to sit, and where Lord Axel sat now. He pointed Kristinn to join him, by taking a seat on the bench at the table, then he waved to one of the ladies who had been serving him earlier, gesturing for her to bring them something to drink.

She nodded and bowed as she went. His Lordship then turned to Kristinn to give him his answer.

"I had no certainty, but I made him an offer that a thief and murderer like him would have a hard time refusing. And since he just recently ambushed and killed two hundred fifty of our men, I knew it would have raised his ego to the point that he would seek more power, and would want to gain more followers. That is why they all had to be killed. Going up against your sovereign is treason, and punishable by death, and now everyone knows that" Lord Axel finished his speech, his face red with anger.

The woman returned to the hall with a small barrel of wine and two cups. They poured themselves some wine, then Kristinn asked the question he wanted to be answered in a low voice since he saw how upset Lord Axel was.

"What did you offer him, my lord?"

"I offered him fifty kilos of gold and told him that he and his men would be pardoned." His Lordship took a sip of the wine. "You did go to his camp?"

"Yes, my lord. We destroyed the camp and captured those he left there. I sent them to Troll Fjord, as ordered. They were mostly women and children. Some of them had been with the outlaws for a long time, others had been captured only a short time ago. They will be returned to their homes, as soon as we get back, my lord."

"Then, there is a matter of state. You will return now, and continue with the work Sir Brian left undone, and that is to build our fleet. We will need as many ships as we can assemble.

"The Ortaks are bringing reinforcement from Orknia to our lands, and shipping out their stolen goods along with their slaves. Those are our people they are sailing away with." Lord Axel frowned. "We must put a stop to them as soon as we can." Now he paused for a while, thinking.

"I will grant you two hundred men for the law enforcement in Troll Fjord and King Forest. The rest of the men, along with the wounded, will join me as I head for Kings Rock within two days. But I will garrison twenty men here at the castle, for patrol by the villages at the lakeside and the surrounding area, and for law keeping. Furthermore, we need to build roads. We should start with a road from Kings Rock to Troll Fjord, through Kings Forest.

"With increasing traffic between those two places, we need to secure safety. I will give you a written command for those matters before you leave," said His Lordship, then he stood, indicating their meeting was over.

Kristin did not reply. That young man has come a long way, but he seems to know what he's doing. I admire that, he thought as he bowed his head and walked outside.

Lord Axel stepped outside into the bailey. His thoughts were elsewhere as he took to the steps upon the castle's rampart. He looked across the lake, to the mountains in the East. He heard his officers shouting and giving orders to their men as they piled the outlaws' corpses to be burned.

That was an unpleasant but necessary measure, so there would be no outbreak of diseases amongst the people.

However, that was not what His Lordship was thinking of at this time. He was worried because of the news that his queen had been receiving from Serpenia.

His sister was in charge of Little Creek and the building of the royal fleet there, and at the same time, she had to deal with outlaws and rebellion amongst the remaining noblemen.

His mother had decided to stay in Goat Valley, along

with many of those he left there a year and a half ago, and he had no way of protecting her from where he was now.

Jacob was handling things well in Finnwood Castle, and Crown City was in good hands, with Commander Erik in charge. And from the report they had, the Ortaks who were given the freedom and opportunity to work as law enforcement proved to be the right choice and were now loyal servants to the queen. That had been a bold move for Captain Jeff, now the governor of Serbia. A smile came across Axel's face when he thought of his friend.

How things had changed since they crawled off the battlefield in Broad Valley, trying not to get killed by the Ortaks.

Then his mind took him to Gunther the farmer and his family, and Lisa. He had not seen them since he left them in Goat Valley.

His heart felt warm when he thought about her, and he remembered her smile, and how beautiful she was, and the smell of her hair when she sat beside him on the cabin's porch the day before he rode away from Goat Valley. He wondered if she still thought about him. Where are they now?

Then his thoughts took him to Erinstein Castle, and Helga, Lord Grimstein's widow, and her two young daughters. Jeff did not talk about them in his reports, but he knew Jeff to be a good man, and he hoped that they would find comfort with each other.

His thoughts were interrupted when one of his officers could be heard giving some of his soldiers a piece of his mind. He turned his head to take a look, but there was nothing taking place that he wanted to put his mind to.

He turned his back again, looking over the peaceful lake. The news they had received from Hergia had troubled him.

Hergia had not answered the call for help when Sir Brian sent a messenger when the Ortaks landed in Salmon Fjord. They did not want to get involved, but now, when they were being invaded by Vikings in the North, and the Ortaks in the South, they sent a representative to Queen Egny's court to ask for assistance.

They were too late for a friendship now, and even so, the queen had sent most of her army south to Eniktronia and could spare no more.

He was relieved when he met up with the representative from the Viking king, to discover that King Haldor The White had no intention of invading Otanga or any of Queen Egny's lands. That was good news, at least for now. And hopefully, a treaty with the Vikings could help them in the future.

Lord Axel waited at the castle until his men had buried the ashes and cleared the area of the outlaws' remains, then he headed off to Kings Rock again, leaving twenty of his men to garrison Easel Castle. They were all good men from this part of Otanga. The kingdom needed people to feel safe again.

He had said goodbye to Kristinn the lawman the day before, and he watched him as he rode off to Troll Fjord with two hundred men. A cold spring shower hit His Lordship's face as he rode through the villages and headed up the slopes, taking the same path as when he arrived at Easel Castle.

~

Most of that winter, King Haldor's men worked on building and strengthening the ramparts around his stronghold, or Kingsburg as his men had named it in honour of their king.

He received reports from his scouts, informing him of the Ortaks invasion on Hergia by crossing White River, and the siege of Castor Castle.

His ships returned, reporting that Queen Egny was having a royal fleet built in Troll Fjord, and another fleet in Little Creek.

He learned from the people in the villages that the valleys by the North coast were often raided by gangs of outlaws from Kingwood, and the noblemen who were supposed to protect the people by the orders from their king in Raven Rock had neglected their duty to do so, but not when it came to tax collecting. Their men showed up for that duty every time.

So, King Harold, had his men build outposts at the East side, on the outskirts of Kingwood. They were raised there to keep law and order, and by doing so, the king hoped to gain some loyalty from the people living in the northern valleys.

He knew that the only way for him to establish his kingdom here in the valleys, was to uphold law and order, so the people would feel safe under his rule, and then they would accept him as their king, welcome him, even.

After defeating the Ortaks in Salmon Fjord, the king received half of the valuables taken at the Ortaks stronghold by Oskar and his men, as they were accustomed to.

It was in mid-winter that a representative from Queen Egny in Otanga arrived on a ship.

King Haldor granted him a hearing and welcomed him

to his house. After the king had a long conversation with the Queen's representative, and after receiving gifts from the queen, he listened to his proposal of a treaty, which he accepted. He made his decision that he would send Her Majesty a senator to represent him at the queen's court in Kings Rocks.

He chose one of his advisers, Gretar, a good man and a great adviser to him for many years. He gave him one of his ships to sail to Troll Fjord, along with a crew and three servants.

During that winter, the king travelled between villages and towns in the North valleys that he had claimed as his kingdom.

He wanted the folks to get to know him and respect him and his laws, but not to fear him.

Winters in the northern valleys could be hard, and snowstorms were a common thing in these parts, but the king and his men were used to that kind of weather, so that did not stop his travels.

More than once, he had to dwell in villages, waiting for a storm to calm down, and that gave him the opportunity to get to know the people.

In one of the villages, he learned that law enforcement from King Oswald was not to be relied on. Those noblemen, mostly lords from the local castles who were supposed to keep up the law, were usually busy minding their own, so thievery and even killing were not investigated or punished by the nobles. They were generally at the king's court in Raven Rock.

There were six small castles in the northern valleys, and when the Vikings landed, most of those living in those castles fled, afraid that the Vikings would attack the castles, so they now sat empty.

Most of them were not functional military structures, just stone houses raised for their masters. They would never have stood a chance against the Viking Army. And the Vikings had no intention of using them for themselves.

It did come as a surprise to King Harold, that King Oswald did not break the siege at Castor Castle, nor did he attack the Ortaks by White River.

Why is he doing that to his men? Why is he keeping almost all his army at Raven Rock? He learned from the people how unpopular the king and his son were, and that he had less trust among his men, than he may realise.

It may be that King Oswald intended to attack the Vikings here in the northern valleys during the winter.

Whatever it was, King Haldor decided to double the scouts and the guards at the outposts west of Raven Rock Mountains, in case King Oswald decided to launch a war.

But nothing like that happened through the winter, and come the following spring, his people ploughed and sowed larger fields than had ever been done before in Hergia.

They were going to get as much food for the next winter as the land could give them. For the newcomers, these were fertile lands, and they were happy.

They were here to stay.

THE WORLD OF ESTHOPIA

Eniktronia

Their king was Haakon; his queen was Sigfrid, sister of Anton, King of Antonia. They have no children. Brother, Prince Cormack, married Sigrid, daughter of King Agnar of Serpenia. She died in childbirth, giving life to a daughter, Egny, twenty-two years of age. King Haakon's youngest brother is Prince Reynard, Duke of Flag Stronghold. King Haakon, along with his brothers, died in the battle at Broad Valley.

The capital of Eniktronia is Eniktronia Castle.

MONTANIA.

Their king was Edward; his queen was Maria, daughter of King Agnar of Serpenia. Their children are: Sigrun at the age of fourteen, Julia, at the age of twelve, and Eyrun at the age of nine. King Edward died in the battle at Broad Valley.

The Capital of Montania is Brandholm.

Serpenia

Their king was Agnar; his queen is Jofrid, and their children Prince Fredrik of Serpenia, and Queen Maria of Montania. With his former wife, Princess Marie of Otanga, he had a daughter, Sigrid. She married Prince Cormack of Eniktronia. She died giving birth to Princess Egny. King Agnar, along with his son, Prince Fredrik, died at the battle at Broad Valley.

The Capital of Serpenia is Crown City.

Antonia

Their king is Anton; his queen is Hilda. Their children are Henry, twenty years of age, and Janus, nineteen years of age. King Anton's sister is Sigfrid, Queen of Eniktronia.

The Capital of Antonia is Crystal City.

Otanga

Their king was Ragnar, a widower; his son is Prince Sigvin. He also had a daughter, Marie, who became queen of Serpenia, mother of Sigrid, mother of Egny. King Ragnar and his son were ambushed and killed.

The Capital of Otanga is Kings Rock.

Hergia

Their king is Oswald; his wife is Gunnfrid. Their son is Gunthor.

The Capital of Hergia is Raven Rock.

Alfheim

Arthenth:
Captain in the Elven Army.

Ethan:
King of Alfheim.

Grisgeir:
King of the barbarians

Hilda:
Princess, and King Ethan's daughter.

Star:
Warrior from barbarian lands.

Tania.
Part Elven. A princess, and a commanding general in the Elven Army.

Ylva:
Warrior from barbarian lands.

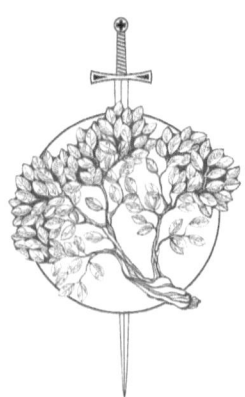